Praise for
Mistaken Identities

"An interesting premise with some unexpected twists."

"I look forward to reading more of each author's works."

"Well written and full of romance and suspense."

"Hoping this series has more books in the works and looking forward to reading them!"

Mistaken Identities

Past. Present Future.

Bambi Lynn

Lesia Flynn

Amy Boyles

Published by Bourdeilles Books

ISBN – 978-0-9914431-9-2
eBook ISBN – 978-0-9914431-9-2

Cover Design by Wicked Smart Designs

Table of Contents

Mask of the Highlander

A Highland Romance

by

Bambi Lynn

Bambi Lynn

ABOUT THIS BOOK

Ty Voss is returning home after years fighting
the English in France. He is anxious to return to
his beautiful wife and finally meet the daughter
he has never known.

Kenna dreads her husband's homecoming like
the plague. The man she married is a cruel
tyrant. She had prayed he would be killed in the
fighting, freeing her from a life of brutal torment
and a loveless marriage.

But the man on her doorstep is not the same.
This man is kind, gentle and sparks a fire in her
she never felt in the early days of her marriage.
Could he be an imposter?

MASK OF THE HIGHLANDER

Bambi Lynn

for Cliff,
as always

And for my Mom,
who always encouraged me
to follow my dreams

Also to Lesia and Amy
I couldn't have done this without you!

CHAPTER ONE

Highlands of Scotland, 14th Century

Kenna waited on the stoop. She gripped her cloak beneath her chin with one hand, shivering in the chilly air. Despite the cold, the sky was exceptionally sunny for such a dismal day. She tried to swallow, but her mouth was drier than *Innis Cheith* in summer. She clenched her other fist so hard her ragged nails drew blood in her palm, a wasted effort to calm her quaking nerves.

He was almost home.

The day she had dreaded for the past five years had arrived. Her husband's party had been spotted on the road from Inverness.

Cold dread settled in the pit of her stomach. *Lord, I beg you. Make his horse stumble. A painless snap of his neck as he hits the ground.* Even as she let the fantasy wash over her, she knew it would not happen. She had prayed fervently that her husband would never return. Men died in battle every day. Was it too much to ask that God send that devil of a man back to hell?

The sound of thundering hooves reached her before she saw him. The rhythmic thump matched the pounding of her heart. She wanted to run, to find a safe place to hide.

But she knew there was no such place.

He crested the hill, followed by half a dozen men. They tore across the knoll, churning up the earth, and through the gates of Castle Vass. People gathered round to greet the men. They were met with hugs, kisses, squeals of excitement and tears for those who had not returned. But most shied away from Ty Vass. Those who had not felt the lash of his tongue, or his fist, had heard tales that would give a bairn nightmares. The rest knew only too well the danger of drawing the laird's attention.

The men continued to dismount, handing off their horses to boys who led them away toward the stables. Ty sat unmoving on his stallion. Thus far, Kenna had looked everywhere *except* at him but she could avoid it no longer. If he decided she had humiliated him, his punishment would be harsh indeed.

She pulled her shoulders back and took a deep breath before she snapped her eyes to his.

To his *eye*.

The other was covered with a black patch. Now he looked as ominous as his brutality proved him to be. Kenna tried to hide her shock, but fear welled up inside her. When his full lips spread into a smile, she almost feinted where she stood.

He stared back at her, that sardonic grin frozen into place. Much of one side of his face obscured by the patch, but it failed to completely mask his hard features. The breeze caught his long black hair, lifting in a swirl of darkness that matched his homecoming. Kenna laced her fingers in front of her, squeezing tight and praying for strength.

He lifted one leg over his stallion, ensuring his red and black plaid did not entangle with the saddle, and jumped to the ground. Robby, a boy of fewer than ten winters, reluctantly trudged over to retrieve the reins. Ty reached for his head with a grin.

Robby ducked, one hand held up in defense.

Ty's smile changed instantly to a frown as he ruffled Robby's hair. The boy looked up at him, wary and skittish, his small hand outstretched. Ty handed the reins over to him and watched with a troubled expression as he hurried away.

When Robby had disappeared, Ty turned his attention to her. Kenna took a step back, but then forced herself to remain still. She would not cower. He had beat her, cursed her, raped her for three days, consummation of their pact, he claimed. The Munro had forced him to marry her, and Ty Vass had promised to make her suffer for it until the end of his days.

Or hers.

Her own clan chief had made the same demand of her, a last effort to avoid an all-out war between Clan Munro and Clan Mackintosh. She had agreed with an open mind and an open heart. She, as much as anyone, wanted to avoid more fighting between the two clans. She had lost three brothers, and an uncle. Enough had died.

However, she had not reckoned with her betrothed's sadistic nature. He was the devil, an evil brute of a man who enjoyed the pain of others. Kenna had cowered enough during the three days following their wedding. Then he left, praise the Lord. For five years he had been fighting the English in France. Five glorious years during which time she had born a child, increased her husband's income and grown to love his people. As much as she had suffered for those three days, many of the people at Castle Vass had had a lifetime of him.

She was no longer the pitiful young waif he left broken and full of despair. She had agreed to marry him to protect her people. Now she would also look after his. They deserved peace, as well. For the sake of her family and his, she would honor this…marriage. She would see it through if it meant peace between their clans. She would not let him intimidate her further. She would stand up to him, fight back no matter what it cost her.

She was not foolish enough to deliberately provoke him though. It had taken weeks for her to mend after he had left. If not for Mrs. Dingwell, she might not have recovered at all. His abuse had been that severe.

Kenna shivered as a sob bubbled up in the back of her throat. Determined to make the best of it she may be, but she was more frightened of him than she wanted to admit.

Swallowing her fear, she met his gaze. He crossed the bailey with a slight limp. She could only hope it was from an injury that would pain him for the rest of his life, which she would continue to pray would not be long.

The gentle smile he pressed on her as he drew closer did nothing to ease her anxiety. She had seen that smile before and knew it hid evil beyond measure. He stopped at the bottom of the stoop and looked up at her with his good eye. Kenna stared back at him, reminding herself not to be afraid. He would not kill her, of that she was certain. Such an action would bring down the wrath of Clan Mackintosh, a price Ty Vass could ill afford. The Munro had threatened to take away all Vass lands if Ty did not make this work.

They each had much to lose without the other. Was that marriage? It certainly was not what she had dreamed of as a girl.

"Do ye no' have a kiss for yer husband, lass?"

***

Kenna swallowed the bile that rose to her mouth and dropped down the two steps to stand before him. With him still on the ground, they met almost eye to eye, but he was so tall, she still had to look up at him. She trembled uncontrollably now.

MASK OF THE HIGHLANDER

He wrapped his cruel hands around the upper part of her arms. "Yer shiverin, lass." He rubbed her arms vigorously through the thick wool of her cloak. "I doona recall having such an effect on you." His lazy smile turned her stomach.

With a gentleness that contradicted his cruelty, he pulled her to him with agonizing slowness. Kenna curled her lip as she drew closer. She closed her eyes and tried to imagine that he was someone else. Anyone else. Old Angus the pig farmer would have been better. Ty's warm breath made her want to retch, not that it was unpleasant. The scent of cinnamon wafted up to her as his lips touched hers.

She expected the sudden urge to heave, not the fiery jolt that shocked her right down to her toes. Her body tingled all over, but her mouth...

Her lips parted seemingly of their own free will. The instant they did, Ty plunged his tongue inside. The courtyard disappeared, leaving them alone even though the bailey still teemed with people. Kenna kept her fists clenched at her sides. Ty's grip on her upper arms was firm, but not painful. He pulled her closer still until her breasts pressed against his chest. A groan rumbled from deep inside him, vibrating against her own pounding heart.

Kenna let her eyes slide open to be sure it was him, stunned at the emotions roiling within her. His lips were soft, his tongue like velvet gliding across hers. Her breath caught in her throat as excitement threatened to overwhelm her. She was a young girl again, experiencing her first kiss.

But this man was not Gavin. She was not lying amongst the heather in a field overlooking her father's lands. She was at Castle Vass, a veritable prisoner in her enemy's lair. The last time Ty Vass had touched her, there had been no hint of tenderness, only pain and humiliation. He had left her scarred, both inside and out, with a longing to end her life. She might have done just that if not for the baby.

The thought of Isla jolted her back to her senses. She squeezed her eyes shut and tried to pull back from him. To her utter surprise, he let her, keeping a tight hold on her until she remained steady on her feet. She stared at him, unable to read his thoughts but startled by the raw passion in his expression.

That was a look she knew well. The look of her husband overcome with lust and eager to take what he wanted, by force if at all possible. It had haunted her dreams and led her to the parapets more than once. How many times had she stared at the ground from the top of the castle's tallest tower and wondered how much it would hurt when she hit the ground.

Hoping to distract him before he kissed her again, she asked, "How did you lose your eye?" Her voice shook with trepidation.

Ty shrugged and reached up to touch the black patch that covered his injury. "Battle scars, *a ghrá.*" He lifted his hand to her face.

Just like Robby, she instinctively drew away. She regretted it almost immediately. He had trained her well not to pull away from him, but to suffer his abuse unless she wanted it intensified.

He smiled sadly and tucked a wayward curl behind her ear. "Ye need not fear me, Kenna."

The way he said her name sent warmth up the back of her neck. What game did he play? Did he toy with her so she would let her guard down, making the assault she knew was coming that much more enjoyable for him?

She spotted Isla peering from behind Mrs. Dingwell's skirt. *No!* she wanted to scream. Kenna knew she would not be able to keep their daughter from him indefinitely, but she was determined to put it off as long as possible. More than any pain he could inflict on her, she feared what he might do to her baby girl.

She curled her fingers around his arm and urged him up the steps. The bulging muscle there was as hard as stone. She squeezed it gently before she could stop herself. "You must be tired from your journey." Kenna would have rather had a bad tooth pulled with nary a dram of whiskey than be alone with him. But at that moment her greatest concern was drawing him away from Isla.

Ty lifted one corner of his mouth, a seductive gesture that set her heart to racing. He allowed her to lead him up the steps, then followed her inside.

Kenna forced her feet to keep moving, across the fresh rushes covering the floor and down the dark corridor that led to the stairs. Torches had been wedged into the sconces bracketed to the walls on either side, but only a few had been lit. Steeped in shadow, the narrow passage forced them to walk one behind the other. Heat from his body seared her back. She hurried her steps but he kept pace despite the limp, his longer stride forcing him up against her every time she slowed.

Fear gripped her. To be alone with him in such close confinement was worse than any nightmare. Her nerves were drawn so taut, she actually squealed when he grabbed her hips.

Fear of reprisal made her halt instantly. He crashed into her with a soft "umph", the bulk of his chest pressing against the back of her shoulders. With his hands still holding her captive, he lodged himself into the crevice of her backside.

He was hard against her. Kenna noticed a twitch in her core that was completely foreign to her. She blocked it out. She could only imagine his satisfaction if he guessed she was in any way aroused by him.

"I dinna mean for ye to stop, *a ghrá*." He buried his face in her hair, his breath tickling the back of her neck. He took a deep breath, causing her to shiver. "'Tis dark in these halls, and I dread losing ye."

She swallowed hard. His whispered words filled her with a mix of dread and anticipation. With a gentle nudge, he urged her forward. Kenna needed no further encouragement. She rushed ahead, eager to quit the tight passage even though the privacy of his bedchamber would provide little more comfort.

They reached the alcove at the end of the corridor and ascended the stairs. When they reached the landing, he pushed the heavy wooden door open and indicated for her to go before him.

Kenna stared into the dark room she had not entered in five years. It was as though she stood on the threshold of Hell and the devil himself stood there to usher her inside. She could barely breathe past the knot in her throat, but she well knew the punishment for delay. Dragging her feet, she stepped into the room just far enough for him to close the door behind her. The snick of the latch reminded her of a death knell.

"Now," he said, his voice low, menacing.

She closed her eyes and braced herself. *Here it comes.*

"Who is the wee lassie yer trying so hard to hide from me?"

***

Concern for her own well-being fled in a single beat of her heart. He would have to kill her before Kenna let any harm come to her child. It made no difference that he was Isla's father.

Again, she felt him at her back. She fought the unease rippling through her and the quiver of her insides.

"She looks like you," he said, tangling his fingers in her hair and raising the strands to his lips. "Hair the color of a fawn's coat, thick and silky-looking." He continued to rub her curls against his mouth as he circled around to stand in front of her.

Kenna stared at his chest, eye level with her small stature, and refused to look up at him.

He dropped the lock over her shoulder and cupped her throat in the palm of his hand, curling his calloused fingers around the back of her neck. "Skin like the finest porcelain." With his thumb beneath her chin, he shifted her head back, forcing her to look up at him. "Eyes the color of the sea before a storm."

The patch covering his left eye lent him an air of malevolence that bordered on devilry. Surely the man was the spawn of Satan.

"Lips like red velvet." His voice, little more than a whisper now, trailed off as he lowered his head.

Kenna steeled herself. She was doing this to protect her daughter. She would use her body to shield Isla, give in to his sadistic demands if he would promise not to harm her.

"So who is she?"

Kenna did kept her eyes closed. "She?"

"The lassie."

Her eyes snapped open. Fear gripped her heart.

He spoke again before she could respond. "Any fool can see she is yer bairn." He sat on the edge of the bed, lifted one leg and began tugging at his boot. "Do ye ken who 'er father is?"

Kenna drew her shoulders back and chanced a glare at him. "I have been with no other man."

He peered at her with his good eye. "That would make her four...five?" Failing with his boot, he slammed it down on the wood planks with a curse. "She looks to be little more than two. Come and help me."

His seductive manner was gone, replaced by the gruff, easily annoyed brute she recognized.

"She came early," she stuttered. He held his foot out to her and motioned her forward. Kenna hurried over. His wrath would be vicious indeed if he suspected Isla to be the issue of another man.

She took the heel of his boot in one hand and clamped the other across his ankle. The intimacy of the moment surprised her. Her first instinct was to stroke the soft suede, caress his leg as she attended him.

His leg was heavy, powerful. She met his gaze. His irritation was gone. This new, seductive husband of hers stared back at her with something akin to enlightenment. His lips parted. A war of emotion battled within the emerald depths of his naked eye. Had the color always been so striking?

"I have a child?"

His whisper was so soft she almost could not hear him. "If not for Mrs. Dingwell..." She dropped her gaze. She had to be careful. Kenna had a soft spot for Ty's housekeeper, and although she had never seen the two of them together, she suspected the old woman had her own fears of the master. Morna Dingwell had been a bitter enemy of the Mackintosh and anyone associated with him for the whole of her life. Yet, after Ty's abuse left Kenna on death's threshold, she had cared for her, healed her and accepted her into the family. Mrs. Dingwell had been the one to pull her down from that turret time after time.

She had been there when Isla was born, coaxing the lassie out when the babe seemed undecided on when to make her entrance into the world. She had been so frail, Mrs. Dingwell had held her in one hand. She was a master healer. Isla had thrived from the beginning. Yet at the age of four, she looked barely big enough to walk on her own.

"I have a child," he said again.

Kenna pulled off his boot and let it drop to the floor. She nodded, taking his other in her hands. Dragging it off, she dropped it next to the first. She straightened and stepped away from him, out of reach.

She jumped when he shot to his feet, but stood her ground. He paced the room, staring off toward the ceiling and removing his clothes as he did so.

Kenna watched him, wary as a rabbit with a hawk circling overhead. He peeled off his shirt, so dirty and tattered it would go straight to the refuse heap. She swallowed at the sight of his naked chest, thick and covered with a light sprinkling of dark hair. He used his opposite foot to push off his worn boots, then hopped on one foot to remove his trews he had worn for riding. The more he took off, the more she gawked. War suited him. He had grown powerful, lethal. But instead of being repelled, Kenna found herself drawn to him.

He seemed to come back to himself when he discovered he was standing naked in the middle of his room. He lifted one arm, ducked his head and sniffed. "I smell powerful strong, don' ye ken?" He wrinkled his nose and grinned at her. "I'll be needin' a bath. I willna meet me daughter in this state."

***

Ian sat chest deep in a tub of tepid water in the center of the earl's bedchamber. He had fought alongside Ty Vass for three years before an English archer had pierced the earl through the throat with an arrow from three hundred paces. He had not died right away. The mayhem of battle had left him lying in the muck created by torrential rain and the blood soaked field. Ian had broken off the feathered end and pulled out the arrow, but instead of making things better, blood had gushed out the hole faster than he could mop it up.

With his own leg injured, possibly broken, Ian had looked around for assistance. His fellow Scots ignored the casualties as the battle raged on. Many stood on corpses as they fought. It could be hours before anyone came around to collect the dead.

Ian lay there, the desolation he had known all his life fled as he awaited death. Finally, he would belong somewhere. Heaven or Hell, he would have a place to call home. He had grown up on the streets of Edinburgh, orphaned so young he did not even know is family name. He was just Ian.

He had jumped at the chance to fight against the hated English. The army would provide the home, the security, Ian had always longed for. His fellow soldiers were the family he never had.

He been assigned to Earl Vass' retinue right from the beginning. They had fought first at Lussac, then a series of skirmishes that led them to Poitiers. The man was a terrible leader, provoking as much bitterness and resentment from his own men as he would from his enemies.

He struck anyone he deemed weaker, and for the slightest offense. In Ian's experience, folks dinna much care for that. He had learned early on the benefit of an easy smile, a kind word. He could teach Ty Vass a thing or two about how to get people to do what you want.

That did not mean he could not fight. Ian could make anything into a lethal weapon if he needed one. He had made many friends among the people of Edinburgh, learning everything anyone was willing to teach him.

Earl Vass had left him alone for the most part. Ian had to demonstrate his skills right away at Lussac. No doubt, Vass recognized a superior rival.

But there was more.

The uncanny resemblance between Ian and Earl Vass undoubtedly raised the hackles on more than one of his comrades. Highlanders were a suspicious lot. Vass kept clear of Ian, often sending him off to sudden death. But Ian always returned unscathed, ready to fight another day.

Ty Vass had suffered an agonizing death. From what Ian knew of the man, it was no less than he deserved. He took pleasure is the suffering of others, inflicting it himself whenever possible. He mistreated everyone. Even his own men hated him.

Ian had looked over at his nemesis. It was like seeing his own reflection in a pool of clear water. Distorted, sometimes unrecognizable, but the same nonetheless. Hair the color of pitch, eyes as green as the emerald isle, their sheer size. They both stood a head taller than the other men they fought alongside, broad through the shoulders and thick-chested. Either of them could pass for the other -

Ian had caught his breath. He let all other thoughts drift away, making room for the kernel sprouting in his mind. He let it spread and grow until it became a picture in his head, all the pieces swirling into place.

He flipped over onto his stomach, propped on his elbows but keeping his head low. The battle had moved on. He was alone among the dead or dying. He glanced around, squirming from one side to the other surveying the area, searching for witnesses. Satisfied that he was virtually alone, Ian wasted no more time stripping off his own clothes and replacing them with those of Earl Vass.

It took a long time and inflicted no end of torture on his injured leg, but Ian was nothing if not persistent. He was clever enough to figure out how to get what he wanted and determined enough to see it though, even if he had to suffer a little along the way.

With agonizing discomfort, he pushed to his feet, rising like a phoenix, reborn as Ty Vass, Earl of Castle Vass and laird to its inhabitants.

He started when the door opened, drawn from his reverie by his wife as she entered his bed chamber and crossed to the table set beneath the window. She carried a tray which she set down without looking at him. She went to the wardrobe and busied herself digging through whatever was inside.

He flipped the patch down over his left eye and watched her with the other. God, she was lovely. She had changed while she'd been out. The tight fitting smock she had been wearing when he arrived was gone, replaced with a loose, earth-colored…sack. Her luxurious hair had been pulled taut into a bun and pinned at the nape of her neck. It gave him a headache just to look at it.

He smiled. She could try as much as she liked to make herself unattractive, but it would not work. Even if he had not seen her, he had kissed her, and the rush of desire to his groin had been enough to make him want more. Soon enough he would have her naked, all that hair spread out on the bed clothes around her. She would not be able to hide her allure from him then.

He waited until she turned back to him, her arms laden with clothes, then emerged from the tub without warning.

She squealed, dropping the clothes to the floor and her gaze to his naked body. Her eyes locked on his engorged cock. They widened in fear. She covered her mouth with both hands and glanced at the door behind him. No way to escape.

He actually felt sorry for scaring her. She, more than anyone, must have suffered greatly at the hands of her husband.

His hands, he had to remind himself.

It doesna matter, he thought. *The old earl is gone, the new one fair and capable.* It would take time for them to see him as anything other than a tyrant, but time was something he had plenty of.

He gave her his most reassuring smile as he stepped out of the tub. She lowered her hands, refusing to cower before him, but continued to look as if she might dart out of reach at the slightest sign of violence.

He had to admire her bravado. He knew the story. The lairds of Munro and Mackintosh had agreed to the marriage between their clans in an effort to promote peace. Kenna was not the first maiden to been used as a pawn and would have accepted her fate with the grace befitting the granddaughter of a clan elder. She had only been married a handful of days before her new husband led a small army to aid the French.

She must have suffered mightily in those few days if her response to him was any indication.

He padded across the floor, dripping water in a path to where she stood, trembling but not daring to run from him. He said nothing as he reached down to retrieve the clean plaid. He draped it around his hips, tossing the sash over his shoulder.

She still did not move, but nor would she look up at him. Her little chin jutted out in a small show of defiance, but she obviously awaited his command. His cock twitched, the idea of her prepared to do his bidding, albeit reluctantly, enough to drive lust into the heart of a priest.

Images of her suffering sprang unwanted to his mind, dousing his desire and igniting a fury he had never experienced before. What must that bastard have done to make her so afraid of him? He took a deep breath, repressing his anger and masking the turmoil inside with a reassuring demeanor that could calm a skittish doe.

When her curiosity could be held in check no longer, she let her eyes travel slowly up to his face.

Careful not to startle her, he reached out and took her hand. He lifted it toward the window, tracing a path from her wrist to the tip of her longest finger. With aching slowness he brought her palm to his lips and pressed a kiss in the center. He flicked out his tongue, laving it across the once tender skin, hardened now by years of hard work.

He recognized the change in her immediately. Her stance softened; a quiet sigh escaped her lips.

What he did not recognize was the change in himself.

***

He was already harder for her than he had ever been before. No woman had stirred him like Kenna Cleary Vass. But that was not what surprised him. After all, every woman he seduced was better than the one before. He made sure of it. The greater the challenge, the more satisfying the pleasure.

What surprised him was his need to enfold her in his arms and assure her she need never fear another man, to protect her from harm and keep her safe - always. He turned his uncovered eye to her face. Their gazes locked. He glanced back and forth between those stormy eyes trying to read the thoughts hiding behind them, but she kept her emotions carefully guarded, no doubt well aware of the consequences for openly defying him.

A disturbance outside drew her attention. She snatched her hand from his and moved toward the window. She leaned across the table to peer down into the courtyard below.

She sucked in a sharp gasp, lifting her hand to her throat and jerking back from the window. She began to tremble again, raising his own hackles. What new terror was this that frightened her so?

In two strides, he stood next to her. Through the warbled glass, he saw a party of no less than twenty men, none of whom he recognized. An older man rode at the fore, scattering people and animals alike as he entered the gate. He had the air of a man prepared to run down anyone slow enough to encumber his arrival.

"Who is that?" he asked.

Kenna looked at him as if he had suddenly grown a second head. Her slender brows pressed together as she regarded him. She glanced out the window before turning her inquisitive expression back to him. "'Tis your father."

His heart lurched. *Father?* It was one thing to fool the people at Castle Vass. Ty had been chief here for less than a year before marching off to France. He was not intimate with any of his tenants.

But this man had known him his whole life and would surely know his own son. The meeting would be a true test of his skills. If he could fool this man, his position was assured.

He sat down on the foot of the bed and pulled on his boots. "Will ye fetch me a shirt?" Kenna grabbed the one she had dropped and handed it to him. He pulled the sash from his shoulder, donned the white shirt and tucked it into the waist of his plaid.

When he struggled with the belt, she came to his aid. Her demeanor timid and fearful, she gently pushed his hands away and straightened the sash.

Laying it across his shoulder, she moved around behind him.

Ty stood still, ever afraid of startling her. He looked forward to the day he did not have to worry that she would bolt at his slightest movement. Her hands on his back as she adjusted the sash sent a thrill through is body that made him want to toss her onto the bed and remain there with her for the rest of the afternoon.

When he was sufficiently presentable, she stepped away from him, forever out of reach. With a quick nod, he left her there and descended the stairs. He entered the hall to find his father standing there with four other men.

"There is my boy!" The older man met him and slapped him on the back hard enough to knock the wind from most men.

"Greetings, father." Ty busied himself pouring a couple of drams from the decanter on the sideboard. He handed one to his father who tossed it back like spring water and held the empty cup out for more.

Ty downed the contents of his own cup and refilled them.

His father wasted no time getting to the point of his visit. "The Munro has agreed to a union between Mira and his eldest."

Who is Mira? He poured himself another drink. "That is good news. When is the wedding?"

"Not until harvest time. The boy is still with the king and will not return until midsummer."

Ty remained silent, letting the information settle and hoping his father would divulge enough clues to allow him to maintain his ruse. He refilled the other man's drink and waited.

"You will hold a gathering to announce your sister's betrothal to the laird's son." He lifted the cup to his lips and watched Ty over the rim.

My sister. "Why have the gathering here?" Ty asked. His father fixed him with a grin so filled with malice, the tiny hairs on the back of Ty's neck stood up. A tremor of foreboding skittered up his spine.

"You will have your wife write a letter to her grandfather, inviting them to Castle Vass. The family will be more likely to attend a gathering on what they believe to be neutral ground." He leaned forward, lowering his voice to a more conspiratorial tone. "You can shed yerself of that whore, and we will finally wipe out the fucking Cleary's once and for all."

CHAPTER TWO

Kenna watched her father-in-law leave, more relieved than when her husband had left her alone in his room. She had fully expected to be a heap on the floor by now, but thus far he had been benevolent and undemanding.

What was this game he played at? What new level of torment did he have planned?

In the few hours since his return, she had already seen the change in the household. Where everyone normally tiptoed around him, afraid of drawing his wrath, the atmosphere remained much the same as it had been for the past five years since he departed. Had everyone forgotten the vile, evil lord who struck fear into the hearts of his charges?

He might have his people fooled, but not her. She saw through the false smiles, the gentle look in his eye, to the devil beneath. She knew him for the monster he was and reminded herself to stay on guard.

The castle was quiet as she made her way down the stairs and through the corridors to Isla's room. She was determined to shield her from her father, but knew she could not keep them apart indefinitely.

She pushed open the door and froze. Isla sat on the floor, playing with her favorite doll. Across from her sat Ty.

Kenna's heart jumped to her throat. The scene was as non-threatening as it could be, yet the sight of her most feared enemy sitting alone with the person she cherished most in the world almost sent her into a fit of sheer panic.

She forced herself to remain calm. With deliberate steps, she crossed to where Isla sat cross legged on the floor and stood behind her. Isla ignored her, enraptured as she was of her father. She had asked about him often, and Kenna had done her best not to instill fear in her, always hopeful that Ty would never return.

Yet return he had. And now he sat on the floor, completely entranced by the doll Isla held out to him. He was the picture of a doting father.

"Pleased to meet you, Ester."

Isla giggled. "Not Ester. Estrild."

He grinned at her. "Ah. Beg yer pardon, milady."

Kenna leaned over and plucked the doll from his grasp. She handed it to Isla and scooped the little girl up in her arms. Hugging her close and pressing a kiss to her temple, Kenna carried to the door. "Go find Mrs. Dingwell and have her get yer supper." She set her down and nudged her across the threshold.

With a wave at the mountain of man filling the room, she scampered off, clutching her doll and calling for the housekeeper.

Kenna turned back to find him looming over her. Would there ever come a time when she did not feel terrified by his attention?

"She is the most beautiful child I have ever seen," he said. His voice was soft and held a hint of sincerity that would have fooled anyone else. She forced herself not to flinch when he reached out to cup her cheek in one massive hand. "She looks just like you."

Her heart fluttered. He had never said a kind word to her before today. She wanted desperately to believe he had changed, that the man standing before her was no longer the tyrant she had married. But it would take more than a kind word to erase the terror of her wedding night.

Still, she knew better than to refuse him, so she stood still as he caressed her lips with the pad of his thumb. She took a deep breath to ease the sudden tightness in her chest. His touch ignited something within her that made her question her sanity. Her insides quivered, not out of fear but something else. Something that made her want more. Something that made her want him to touch her all over. A slow burn started in the pit of her stomach and spread to the center of her body.

When he took her in his arms and clamped his mouth over hers, she actually leaned into him. She told herself she was only trying not to provoke his anger. He slipped his tongue between her lips, tangling with hers. A moan escaped her, an involuntary reaction to a swell of longing that left her completely baffled.

She hated this man like no other. So why did the possessive crush of his arms, the power of his chest against her hard nipples, the manly scent of him make her want to shed her clothes and feel her naked skin against his?

He kneaded her backside, pressing her throbbing core against the hardness of his shaft. Through the fog of desire clouding her head, she marveled at the size of him, fearing the agony that would come when he took her.

More alarms struck the part of her brain that should be questioning the change in him. The loss of her maidenhead had been excruciating. But the pain had been due to his brutal treatment of her innocence, not the size of his cock.

Doubt fled as he lowered his hand to the juncture of her thighs. The feel of his fingers massaging her through the coarse wool of her skirt drove away all but the most animalistic of thoughts.

The intensity of his kiss doubled. He fumbled with her clothes, dragging the hem up to gain better access to her most intimate spot. He moved her undergarments aside with the deftness of a man well familiar with the workings of a woman's attire. When the calloused tips of his fingers met her naked folds, Kenna exploded in a rush of sensations that made her wrench her mouth from his. She let her head drop back as a cry of exquisite pleasure flooded over her.

Her knees buckled, every muscle melting inside her skin. Ty took the tender flesh of her ear between his teeth and nibbled her softly. He held her upright as spasm after spasm threatened to overwhelm her. "What is happening to me?" Her words came out a ragged whisper as she could hardly breathe. Was she dying?

"I've got you, *a ghrá*."

His voice, gruff and husky with desire penetrated her thoughts. Slowly, Kenna came back to herself. Desire fled as memories of his hands on her small body came rushing to mind. She was alone again, a virtual slave to this man who had caused her so much harm. Something akin to a sob bubbled up in her throat. She pressed her palms to his chest. "Please, don't."

She regretted her words immediately. She had fallen into his trap. He thrived on her pleas for mercy. Kenna fully expected his tender caress to turn into the blows of submission she knew he enjoyed.

She swallowed her fear and braced herself.

***

Ty released her. One thing he had learned over the years was that when a woman said no, no is what she meant. It made little difference what her body was saying.

Already he missed Kenna's wee form against his. Despite the difference in their sizes, she fit him perfectly. He stared down at her terrified face. His heart melted at her fear. It would take time, he knew, to chase away the memories she harbored of the man she thought him to be.

"I am sorry, *a ghrá*, for the way I have mistreated ye. I doona ken exactly what happened between us...before I left." She flinched when he lifted his hand, but he ignored it, rubbing his fingertips against his forehead, as if trying to remember. "War betimes does that to a man, takes away his memories, especially those he would rather forget."

He forced himself not to smile at the look of sheer and utter shock on her face, but to savor the notion that she would forgive him, bury the past and welcome him into her bed. His heart flared in his chest. He cupped her face in his hand, caressing her cheek with the pad of his thumb. "Ye need never fear me again, *a ghrá*. I swear t' ye. I'll not force ye against yer will. I promise."

She relaxed a little, uncertainty and mistrust glowing in her eyes. She let them close, parted her lips.

Her mouth beckoned him to kiss her again. Her breathing increased. The heat of her soft skin warmed his palm. Ty's cock surged with desire. Kenna Cleary was a passionate woman. She just needed the right man to coax that passion from her.

He was that man. And he would savor every moment. The longer it took him to seduce her, the sweeter their lovemaking would be. Then she would be his in more than name only. His *wife*, his beloved, the mother of his child.

His child. He still could not believe it. The precious wee bairn might not have been born of his seed, but he had fallen in love with Isla the moment he set eyes on her. Her slight frame, her mass of curly brown hair, the hint of color in her cheeks. She was the image of her mother. Two women he would protect with his own life and cherish until his last day.

He dropped his hand, surprising her further, and straightened his blasted clothes. The kilt had not been a part of his attire growing up. A simple pair of ragged trews, made of coarse wool that chaffed a man and not the plaid of the highlands, a dingy shirt and the occasional pair of boots riddled with holes had been the extent of his wardrobe. He still struggled to dress himself without drawing suspicion.

"'Tis late," he said. "Mrs. Dingwell promised me supper, I think I shall go and track her down." He glanced around his daughter's room, as awkward as an untried lad with his first whore. "Where do ye sleep?" Except for the days before her husband left, he doubted she had stepped foot inside that bed chamber before today.

Her eyes flitted between him and the door. "I sleep here, with Isla."

He nodded, disappointed. "Verra well. We will ride out in the morning, you and I. I wish to…reacquaint myself with my tenants." He waved a hand at her look of protest. "No rent collecting, mind ye. Just a survey of the land. Five years is a long time."

He moved to the door but turned back to her before leaving. "If ye change yer mind about where to sleep, *a ghrá*," he flashed his most amiable smile, "ye ken where to find me." He gave her a wink so slight she would wonder if she had imagined it and left her gaping after him.

***

They rode out shortly after dawn. The hills were covered in a mist so thick, Kenna could barely see her horse's ears through the fog. The mare shied often at the close proximity of Ty's stallion. The beast, as dark and menacing as his master, snorted and pawed the ground whenever they stopped.

Three starving villages remained on Vass lands. Ty insisted the villagers would want to see their laird, returned home from defeating the English. They had visited each in turn. The arrival of the laird drew the ragged villagers from indoors, but if he expected a hero's welcome, he would be disappointed. The tension in the air was thicker than the fog, each village worse than the one before it. By the time they reached the third, he did not even dismount.

He was cordial enough. His scowl of contempt did not seemed directed at the villagers but at the squalor in which they lived. However, they did not know that. A glower from Laird Vass was enough to strike fear into the hearts of the most stout of men, regardless the cause.

She glanced over at him as he pulled his horse to a halt at the crest of a hill. Her heart tripped. Dare she hope that war *had* changed him? Was he right and truly a different man, or did he play some game to distract her, to lull her into relaxing her aegis. Then he would strike.

He stared off into the distance, beyond the grassy plain toward the border of his lands and her father's. But his gaze was unfocused. Lines of worry creased the corner of his eye, his mouth. She had never known Ty Vass to worry about anything except his own pleasure. His raven-dark hair caught a breeze and swirled around him.

Kenna caught her breath. He had not seemed so handsome before, not when he was beating her, forcing himself on her. Those memories, nightmares she had relived again and again, began to fade. She saw the man he could be, a man she would be proud to call *husband.*

She gave herself a shake. Verra well. She would play along, see how his homecoming played out. Kenna wanted nothing so much as peace in her life. Peace between their clans, and peace within her own house...

...and heart.

"Come." She spurred her mare forward. "I have something to show you."

He did not speak, but Kenna sensed his stallion behind her. Her mare swished her tail overmuch, drawing strange sounds from Ty's war horse. Soon enough she found herself scanning the brush, searching for an opening she had not seen in years. She had last come here on the eve of her wedding. It seemed a lifetime ago.

She paced her mare back and forth along the same gnarl of overgrown vines until she spotted it. "Here." She pulled her leg over the horse's neck and slid to the ground. She knelt in the grass, still damp from the morning's fog and coaxed the vines apart, revealing a wooden door, barely hanging on its hinges.

She grinned over her shoulder at him, but her smile fell instantly. He watched her with a look akin to lust. She hesitated, old fears skittering up her spine, but reminded herself of her vow to give him a chance. She would never trust him, never love him, but by God she would make peace. Besides, there was nothing he could do to her here that he could not do to her elsewhere.

She knew little of his upbringing, but what she did not was enough to turn the heart of any woman who had loved a child. Ty's own mother had died birthing him, a feat his father found pleasing. To have sired such a braw laddie as could rip a woman asunder to take his place in the world. There was a son t' be proud of.

Kenna shuddered to imagine the lessons Ty has been taught growing up. As bad as her husband was, his father was worse.

With a faint smile, she turned away and concentrated her efforts on opening the door. After struggling for several moments, she felt him behind her. His presence engulfed her, trapping her against the massive expanse of his chest.

He reached a beefy arm around her and gave the door a great shove, heaving it into the darkness.

Kenna was fully aware of what lay beyond and had no fear of the close interior. Daylight guided her to a small table where she found flint and a candle, enough to illuminate the inside of the small cottage.

Ty ducked and stepped through the door, filling the inside and staring around in surprise.

Kenna followed his gaze, fully aware that he stood between her and the door. She tried to ignore it, taking in the broken stool, the crockery piled in the corner, the cold hearth. She took calming breaths, using the wobbly table as support. She was trapped in close confinement with him, her grandfather's hated enemy and the man she feared most.

Relief flooded her when he moved from in front of the door and further into the room. *He is changed,* she told herself. *Please, God. Let it be so.* The ice around her heart melted a little when he turned a wondrous smile on her.

"What is this place?"

She took a deep breath and let it out slowly. "I discovered it as a child. It was my secret place." She plied him with a sad smile and shook her head. "I have not been in years."

He circled the room, no more than a few paces with his gigantic stride, until he stood beside her. The door was at her back, so she could still escape if needs be. This time she did not flinch when he lifted his hand.

***

"Thank ye for bringin' me here." He cupped her face in his hand. His gut wrenched when she moved. Did she flinch from his touch or did she snuggle her cheek against his palm? Impossible to discern such a slight movement. He could only hope for the latter.

He glanced quickly from one stormy blue eye to the other, discouraged not to find her innermost thoughts reflected there. She regarded him coolly, allowing him liberties he had every right to claim as her husband but prepared to flit away at the first hint of violence.

He let out his breath in a whoosh. How long before she looked at him with all the passion lurking behind her guarded gaze? He took a step back and surveyed the room. "You've not much in the way of furniture."

She followed his gaze and shrugged. "I saved what I could." She gave him a tentative, lop-sided grin that melted his heart. "I never brought company here before."

He pressed her with a smile intended to put her further at ease. "I am touched that ye would share it with me."

"Ye seemed so…sad earlier. I thought 'twould cheer ye. I used to come here when I was sad. I came just before we -" She stopped abruptly and dropped her gaze to the floor. "- married," she whispered.

Ty barked a laugh, startling her. Her gaze shot to his face and she gripped the table behind her, but she stayed put. "And did it help?"

"I am no longer sad, if that's what you mean."

He tilted his head, regarding her. She did not fidget under his perusal. Slowly, as if approaching an injured wildling, he took a step closer. Kenna squared her shoulders. "What are you now?" He stopped in front of her, close enough to feel her breath on his neck, but not touching.

Her voluptuous chest rose and fell with her deep breaths. "I have been - content at Vass Castle, before you -"

She bit down on whatever she had been about to say. Ty had a good inclination what that was. He leaned over and kissed the top of her head, then the edge of her temple. He lifted her hair over her shoulder, pushing her sleeve down and pressing his lips to the naked skin at the base of her throat. "Before I came home," he whispered into her hair, finishing her thought.

He felt her swallow, a forced move that revealed her discomfort. Her pulse throbbed against his mouth. He trailed his lips along the curve of her shoulder before leaning back and giving her more space.

Her eyes were closed, her luscious lips parted. He let his gaze fall to the soft mounds of her breasts. Her bodice, laced tight on all four sides, pushed them together in a way that made him want to bury his face there and sleep for eternity.

He reached out and drew one finger across them, dipping into the crevice before rising over to trace a path across her creamy skin. She trembled at his touch. She parted her eyes just enough to watch him, ever watchful for sudden movement or a change in demeanor.

"Ye are so beautiful, *a ghrá*." He leaned forward just enough to touch is lips to hers. He made no other move on her, but waited for her breathing to slow, her shoulders to relax. Then he pulled away, tucking a finger beneath her chin and lifting her face up to his. "I cannae change the past, Kenna. I cannae say I'm sorry enough to undo the hurt I caused ye."

He kissed her again, working his mouth against her, hungry for her in a way that surprised him. Even with her staid indifference, he had never wanted a woman more. "Ye can have a good life here, at Vass Castle. We have a beautiful little girl. We can make a home for Isla and all our other bairn, should be we so blessed."

She glared at him with a fire he had not seen before. His heart swelled with pride in her. She was no lowland mouse, cowering to her husband and letting the world walk over her. Not his highland lassie. She was a woman of substance, a true highlander and all that a man could ever want.

"'Tis hard to forget, *m'laird.*"

Her last word held a hint of sarcasm, just to let him know how little respect she had for Ty Vass. He couldn't help but smile. Besides every time he did, the expression in her eyes softened, opened for him just a little more.

She was so vibrant, despite her fear and hatred of him. His longing shocked him to his core. He wanted her naked and panting in his arms, crying out for him as she came. His need for her actually scared him, and he had never been scared of anything.

His entire body hardened urging him to taste those lips that teased but never invited him. He lowered his head to hers, brushing his lips across hers and causing a friction that set his mouth on fire. He growled like a wildling, his desire for her straining for release. Had he let it go unchecked, she might have been justified by her fear.

He cupped her face in his hands, deepening the kiss. Her scent washed over him, bathing him in sensations he rarely allowed himself to entertain. A woman like this could break a man, even one who had never been truly whole to begin with.

He squeezed his eyes tighter, swirling his tongue with hers, tasting her passion which only fueled his own. He ached in places he had never known a man could ache.

"Let me help you forget, *a ghrá.*"

***

What was wrong with her? He was evil and sadistic, hurtful and frightening, and the most lust-worthy man she had ever known. She wanted him to make her forget the man he had been, to prove to her that he was changed, a different man.

Misgiving niggled at the edge of her thoughts, but she had no time to ponder her suspicion as he twined his fingers in her hair and pulled her face up to his. He tilted her head and ravished her mouth with his silky tongue. He licked her lips, nudging them apart and snaking his way inside her.

Kenna rested her hands on his hips. She did not pull him closer, but neither did she push him away. Instead she kissed him back, marveling in the sensations she would never have expected to feel with this man.

Whoever he was.

Again, doubt plagued her, but this time she brushed it aside, preferring instead to remain in the little fantasy she had created inside her head. With him kissing her like this, it was not hard to do. He seemed to pour his entire soul into that kiss. Who was she to deny the attraction between them, the kernel of hope that they could have a pleasant life together?

He reached up and cupped her breast through her bodice. Her nipples hardened, remembering the mind shattering thrill she had experienced yesterday. Would he make that happen to her again? She certainly hoped so. Even now, she could feel the ache building in her core.

Pushing her back over the table, he tugged loose the laces of her bodice, pulling everything over her shoulder and exposing her to the frigid air. Sparks popped behind her eyes as he closed his warm mouth over her painfully hard nipple.

Kenna arched her back, grinding her breast against him. Had she known it would be like this, she would surely have taken a lover by now. She stroked the silky strands of his pitch-dark hair, cradling him against her as she watched him suckle her. The image was nearly enough to send her over the edge.

She lifted his face back to hers. "Ty," she whispered, before kissing him with all the passion she had not known existed within her. He sought the hem of her gown, never taking his delicious mouth from hers. Kenna squeezed her eyes shut. If she looked at him, if she found the cruel expression she so feared, her passion would dissipate. She wanted to know what this was like, she wanted him to show her.

Kenna kicked her feet out of the tangle of her hem, rewarded when he tugged it up her leg. His cold fingers on the warmth of her calf, raised goose flesh all the way up to her shoulders. He gripped her thigh, pushing it off to the side, making it possible to wedge himself between her legs.

She silently praised the convenience of his clothing, but all thought was driven from her brain when he entered her. Pure ecstasy flooded her. She let out a soft sigh as he buried himself inside her. She clasped her ankles around his waist, holding him to her.

Ty dropped his head between his shoulders, his mane a shroud around them hiding them from the world. He pressed his forehead to hers. Kenna still dared not open her eyes. She held him, savored the feel of him, so much different than before. There was no pain, no fear, no humiliation. Only tenderness and longing.

And exquisite pleasure.

She let her head fall back when he began to move inside her, drawing the length from her, sucking out his essence, before plunging to the hilt yet again. Each time he filled her, Kenna opened her mouth to cry out. But each time she bit back her shameless display of wanton abandon.

He emptied into her just as her own world exploded. Kenna wrapped her arms around his chest, her face pressed into the crevice of his bulging muscles, holding on until they were both spent.

Too soon, cold set in. Kenna shivered as he stepped away from her. He pulled her skirt down and readjusted her cloak about her shoulders. She kept her eyes down, but she could not resist a peek when he refitted his kilt.

Nothing about this man repelled her. When she should be disgusted by his proximity, she longed for the comfort and safety of his arms. Where his vile touch should make her cringe, she tingled whenever he came near.

She watched his hands, fascinated at the way they fumbled with his sash. His fingers were strong, yet they made her skin spark and crawl in a pleasant way. His touch was possessive, yet gentle beyond reproach, as if he took pains to thwart her unease.

It was no mystery to Kenna that a man's countenance, his demeanor could grow over his life. That he could soften. Perhaps he had even found God.

But could a man change *so* much?

She could not stop herself from trying to peer beneath his plaid. She tried to recall the memories she had worked so hard to block out over the past five years. Her determination had paid off. She could hardly remember any details about her husband's physical appearance. Still, Ty Vass was hiding a lot more beneath his kilt that the man who had marched off to France.

What did they feed men in France that could make them…grow like that?

CHAPTER THREE

Ty watched his wife scurry around the room, tidying up the floor and driving dust balls into a pan. The past few days had been bliss for him. Since that day in the cottage, she had relaxed somewhat. She was not completely at ease, yet neither did she seem like she would flit away at the slightest disturbance.

Except when they were in this room.

Even if he was not touching her, he could feel her tense whenever she entered, and she was a wary as a trapped bird while she was there. Their love-making was not the passionate tumble of that day. Instead, her demeanor was that of someone standing on the edge of a cliff, preparing to jump to their doom. Again he wondered what her husband had done to her and wished the man were alive so he could kill him.

His wife had come to mean a lot to him since his return. *His wife.* Ty smiled. He love the way that felt on his lips. So much more than the comely wench he had expected to find. Her biting sarcasm could cut a man off at the knees. He had seen her get more work out of his soldiers than he had witnessed from them during months of living rough in France. But there was no mistaking the succor she gave to his people. She could comfort a crying child, lend support to a grieving widow and manage his household staff with little more than a word and an appropriate expression. She lightened the mood whenever she came around. Her sense of humor had even piqued old Angus the pig farmer. It was reported he never so much as cracked a smile except for the laird's wife.

His heart softened as he watched her. *Ye need never fear another man,* a ghrá, *not as long as I draw breath.* It shocked him at times, how much he cared for her, how much he wanted to please her. He flushed each time she smiled, even though her face had yet to light up on his account. He vowed to change that.

"There seems a mighty draft in this room. D' ye feel it?"

She turned startled eyes to him. "A draft?" She glanced around, her lip turned up slightly as she surveyed the room. "Shall I add wood to the fire?"

He shrugged and continued dressing. "I would prefer another room, I think. One not so isolated from the rest of the castle." He watched closely for her reaction.

At first she gave none. Was her surprise so great? Her shoulders slumped a little and the worry lines etching her beautiful face softened. "A different room?" Her voice was barely more than a whisper.

He pulled on his boots and stomped them on the floor, driving down his heel and cramming his toes deeper inside. He winced at the pain. He had to have new boots made.

"Unless you prefer this one. It does give us much privacy." He waggled his brows at her but failed to illicit the light-hearted response he had hoped for.

She shook her head vigorously. "Not at all. The old solar is almost never used. Mrs. Dingwell stores linens in there, I believe. It would make a lovely chamber for the laird of the castle. Should I have Mrs. Dingwell start fixing it up for you?"

Her excitement grew as she talked. Ty was glad. Perhaps once they were settled in the new room she would relax a little, let down her defenses and release the passionate woman he knew she held in check. He gave her his most seductive smile and crossed the room to her.

Taking her in his arms he kissed her long and hard. He could not get enough of kissing her. The feel of her lips. The sweet taste of her, like honey dripping of a slice of freshly baked bread.

He was pleased that she returned his kiss with something akin to desire. It was the first time she has shown such enthusiasm since they day the visited the dilapidated cottage. He made a mental note to seek out other things that would please her.

He pulled away reluctantly. "I cannot linger, *a ghrá*. I promised Angus I see to the building of a new pig sty. I look forward to spending this night in our new room. You will see to the details?" She beamed up at him, a smile that made his heart melt.

He had to leave before he tossed reason to the wind and spent the remainder of the day in bed with her. Old Angus could wait. He appeased himself with thoughts of coming home to her, his wife, and sleeping with her nestled in his arms, wrapped in the bed clothes beneath the roof of their new room. One they would share. It would be the beginning of a new life for them.

As happened every time he let himself imagine the happiness they would share, worrisome thoughts of his *father* and his plan to become laird of Clan Munro seeped into his musings. How was he going to save Kenna's family and prevent an all-out war? The gathering was little more than a fortnight away. He was running out of time and thus far, no suitable plan had come to him.

Other than slipping away and killing the old man under the darkness of night. But even that would be blamed on the Clearys. He needed to come up with a plan to redirect his father from his diabolical scheme.

If his sister was to marry the Munro's son, her offspring would become laird. Somehow, Ty had to convince his father to be satisfied that his own grandson would one be laird of Clan Munro. Ty's children would rise high among the ranks of clan Mackintosh, as well, thanks to Kenna's lineage.

And best of all, there would be peace between the clans for the first time in living memory.

Ty shook his head. Solutions were abundant but no path was forth-coming. It gave him a headache to think about it. He kissed the tip of her nose. "I look forward to sleeping," he kissed her lips, "or not sleeping," he winked at her, "in the love-nest you will create for us this day." She blushed all the way to the tips of her ears, making him laugh as he limped across the floor.

Just as he reached the door, he turned back at a muffled sound from her. She watched him, arms crossed, her tongue pressed to the inside of her cheek, suspicion and doubt riddling her features.

"Leg botherin' ye, m'laird? Or did ye're boots shrink while ye were away?"

**

Kenna stretch like a cat waking from a nap, tangling herself among the rumpled bedclothes and refusing to open her eyes. If she kept them closed a little longer, she could pretend she did not have so much work to do. Perhaps Mrs. Dingwell would allow her to stay abed.

She reached over, disappointed to find her husband already gone. He had said he would rise early to help the men with the new gate house. She was surprised the disturbance did not wake her. She was a light sleeper most nights, but she supposed after their exuberant bedplay the night before…

Kenna buried her face in her pillow. She should be embarrassed by her wanton enthusiasm. Since Ty had moved out of his old room a sennight ago, she had held little in reserve, showing more and more fervor each night they spent together. Her relief at being out of his chamber of horror was that liberating. He had even gone so far as the seal up the corridor that led to it. She had been touched by his efforts. She still did not trust him, but for the first time in five years, she could envision a happy future, not one filled with dread.

She pulled his pillow against her chest, inhaling his scent. Her heart fluttered inside her chest, giving her a little thrill. She wished he had slept in this morning, as well.

What an odd thought. A week ago she considered killing her husband with her own hand. Now she actually longed for his company, anticipating the time they would spend together at the end of the day. He would come in from whatever project he had been working on, seeking her out immediately before hunting down his wayward daughter, who was never where she was supposed to be. Thank God for Mrs. Dingwell. Otherwise Isla might be lost and never seen or heard from again.

Aye, things had certainly changed at Vass Castle. Everyone was so much more relaxed, she and Mrs. Dingwell had to keep after everyone to see that all the work was done. And there was so much to do. There had not been a gathering in years, and nothing in the way of fun at Vass Castle since…well, ever.

Add to that the fact that this would be the first gathering of Clan Munro that included members of Clan Mackintosh. Everyone was so excited, it was hard to get any work out of them at all. Again she realized how much she relied on Mrs. Dingwell. The woman could light a fire under the laziest youth or the most stubborn old man. The woman knew how to get people moving.

Kenna groaned and hugged Ty's pillow tighter. The housekeeper would be lighting *her* fire if she did not get up and put herself to work. Still…if she could allow herself a few more minutes….

…a few more minutes to think about her husband. *Her husband.* She wondered again how a man could change so much. The only similarity was his appearance. Yet even that was vague at times. The patch he wore over his eye hid much of his face making it difficult to recall the evil visage of the man who had stood next to her at her marriage. Her relief at finding Ty Vass a virile young man, his appearance more than pleasant, had been quickly shattered by his brutal treatment of her on their wedding night.

His stature was the same. His hair, night-black waves that fell in a sheet down his back, was also unchanged. The size of his man part was definitely bigger. Did a man continue to grow after reaching adulthood? Kenna could not say, but perhaps it was possible. He had had to commission new boots because the only ones he had that fit were the ones he had worn on the journey home.

No, there was something more, something he was hiding from her. He was different on the inside. He showed genuine concern for everyone, always greeting his vassals with a kind word, a complement or praise for a job well done. He took time to laugh with the children, or teach the young lads the ways of men, demonstrating a technique with the sword or the best way to handle a horse. He teased Mrs. Dingwell so much she now blushed whenever he entered the room. His easy way with Isla, his ready smile, warmed Kenna's heart.

What had happened to him while he was in France? Had the horrors of war made him recognize his own brutality? Had he faced death and vowed to change his ways if God spared him? Unlikely. Mayhap he had met a woman.

The thought of her husband with another woman ignited a different kind of fire within her. Fury, rage, and she was surprised to admit, jealously. Emotions she would never have expected to feel over the infidelity of Ty Vass.

Could this man be an imposter?

Her eyes shot open. Could that be it? She thought harder, trying to narrow her suspicion. The patch over his eye…she tried to recall if she had seen him without it since his return. He kept it firmly in place at all times, except when he slept. Even then, he did not take it off until all the candles had been extinguished and the room was bathed in darkness.

She needed a trap. She immediately questioned that idea. If the man who shared her bed was truly an imposter, did she really want to know? There was no doubt that she was better off, everyone was. Could God have answered her prayers and smote her husband on the battlefield, sending her a guardian angel to take his place? If He did, who was she to question His will?

Would her own curiosity allow her to ignore her suspicions? Doubtful.

Kenna rose with new determination. Tossing back the covers, she padded naked across to the window and opened the shutters. Morning light streamed in along with a chilly breeze. She grabbed a robe and pulled it around her shoulders then, leaning against the window embrasure, she searched the courtyard for the distinct form of her husband.

When she spotted him, her heart tripped. He *had* to be an imposter, for she had never felt about her husband the way she felt about this man.

***

MASK OF THE HIGHLANDER

Two days before guests were expected to start arriving, Ty finished the gate house. He stood with his men, surveying the work. He noted the workmanship, the refinements they had made. He issued praise where it was justified and noted possible problems they would need to keep an eye on.

But his thoughts were elsewhere. He had not seen Kenna even though it was already past noon. Today was his wife's birthday, and he had a special surprise for her.

The final inspection complete at last, he rushed back to the keep. Mrs. Dingwell had promised to have him a bath waiting, so he wasted no time getting to it before the water grew cold. A hot bath was one luxury he took advantage of every chance he got. As a child living on the streets of Edinburgh, he seldom had a bath at all, much less a hot one. He had first discovered the pleasure of heated water at a brothel outside Paris and vowed to never take a cold one again.

He smiled at the steaming tub as he pushed open the door to his chamber. He stripped naked, leaving a trail of discarded laundry, and stepped into the warm water. He slid below the surface with a contented sigh. He noted the basket of provisions, another gift from Mrs. Dingwell. Bless her. This was going to be a glorious day.

Half an hour later, his day got even better. Kenna walked into the room, filling the space with her presence and stirring the beast in his gut despite the dropping temperature of the water. He was glad his cock was submerged as he was still wary of frightening her, and she seem particularly guarded when it came to his size. He and Ty Vass had been alike in so many other ways. Was their endowment so different?

"We missed you at table, m'laird," she said as she set clean linens on the bed.

He took the drying cloth she handed him and stood. "Aye. The gate house needed a final inspection and now there is even more business to attend. No time for luxuries like eating," he joked.

"Are you off then?"

A prickle of pleasure skittered up the back of his neck at her seeming disappointment. The very idea that she missed him when he was gone warmed him from the inside out. No one had ever missed him. He nodded and pulled her against his damp, naked skin.

Kenna stepped into his arms without hesitation. How far she had come since his return a fortnight ago. There was still a small part of herself she held in check, and she watched him with an air of mistrust a blind man could see. But the fear was gone from her warm brown eyes. When he touched her, she trembled from desire instead of the terror she had shown in the beginning.

Pressing a kiss to the top of her head, he eased her away and reached for his discarded kilt. "There are some things I need to take care of in one of the outlying villages. Will you accompany me?"

She look startled. "I…there is much still to do before the guests start to arrive. How long will you be gone?"

"We shall be back by supper tomorrow. Mrs. Dingwell can see to the preparations until then."

She smoothed her hair and glanced around. "I would have to gather some…and change my clothes."

Ty finished dressing and picked up the basket Mrs. Dingwell had left for him. "Yer clothes are fine, *a ghrá*. Ye're as lovely as a lassie on Bealltainn." He smiled when she blushed. He pulled her cloak from the peg on the wall and, handing her the basket to hold, placed it around her shoulders. He took the basket back from her, grinned at her expression of confusion and held his arm out toward the door. "Shall we?"

***

It was late afternoon by the time they arrived at the cottage. The door was nearly impossible to find amidst the overgrowth, even to one who knew where it was. Ty halted his stallion nearby and helped Kenna down from her own horse.

She eyed him with the suspicion that had been growing steadily since they passed the first village. She had made no comment as they skirted the ramshackle huts, but her cheery prattle had diminished considerably. By the time they passed the second, she had clammed up like a mute and said nary a word. Since leaving the third village behind them, she had made no effort to hide her uncertainty.

Ty would have found her wariness endearing had he not known the source, but at least she did not cower from him in fear. The hate and loathing she had shown at his homecoming was gone, leaving only doubt and caution. He could not be more proud than to have a wife of such strength as Kenna Vass.

She stood there, looking back and forth from him to the hidden door. "What are we doing here?"

Her voice trembled. Ty ached to soothe her concerns, but nothing he could say would accomplish that. Soon enough she would trust him, and if not sooner, then later.

He smiled and jerked his head toward the mass of brambles that hid the cottage. "I have something for you…inside." He reached through the brush and pushed the door open. Without waiting, he went inside and began lighting candles. By the time she joined him, the room was bathed in a soft glow that revealed a hideaway very different from the one they had visited the last time.

Kenna stopped just inside the threshold, a gasp of surprise the only sound in the small cottage. Ty busied himself starting a fire in the hearth, giving her time to look around. He squatted before the fire, staring at the growing flames. He ached to see her face, to know if she was pleased with what he had done.

He tensed when he felt her behind him. His body was already so hard for her. His craving surprised him at times. He was like a man starved, and she the only sustenance that could satisfy him. His skin tingled when she placed her hand on his shoulder.

"You did this?"

He stood, towering over her and filling the small room. *"Lá breithe shona dhuit,"* he whispered.

She frowned at the phrase. "It's my birthday?" He nodded. She looked around with newfound surprise. "And all this…is for me?"

'All this' was a complete transformation of the sanctuary she had escaped to as a child. Gone were the few pieces of broken furniture, the cobwebs, the decades of dirt and neglect. The place had been scoured until nary a ball of dust remained, even the tiny window allowed in a scant amount of the remaining sunlight. The dilapidated furniture had been replaced with a table, two short stools and a bed frame, a fresh inviting tick atop the floorboards. A bundle of primroses filled a vase in the middle of the table, filling the room with a spicy, comforting fragrance that reminded Ty of spring.

He smiled down at her. "I suppose fairies must have fixed the place up since the last time ye were here." He took her hand and lifted it to his mouth, pressing a soft kiss to her palm. "D'ye like it, then?"

Tears sparkled on her lashes, and he could tell she had trouble speaking. He almost laughed. That must be a first. She laid her palm against his cheek, smoothing the patch that covered his eye and staring deep into the other one.

"No one has ever done anything like this for me. Thank you."

He cocked his eyebrow at her, pressing her with his most devilish grin. "I hope ye have some other way of showin' yer thanks?"

She looked up at him from beneath lowered lashes, her lips cocked into a saucy grin. "Ye can bet I do." She sank to her knees, clasping his naked thighs beneath his kilt and running her hands up to squeeze the cheeks of his arse.

Ty sucked in his breath, surprised and delighted. He had not expected such an intimate expression of gratitude. But he welcomed it nevertheless.

Ty groaned in pleasure as she kneaded his backside. Her dainty hands made goose flesh rise on his thighs as she slid the tips of her fingers around the sensitive skin of his hips. He squeezed his good eye shut, afraid of coming too soon. He wanted to savor this, imagine he could stay here with her forever. The vision of her, selfishly pleasuring him, made him yearn, just once, for someone to love him.

She squeezed his shaft in a delicate grip, cupping and kneading his sac with her other hand. She released him and fumbled with the hem of his kilt. It was all he could do not to cry out when she took him into her mouth.

He gasped in shock. No one had ever done this to him before. He held his breath. The pleasure of her warm mouth engulfing his cock, her delicate lips squeezing around him, pulling him deeper and deeper into her, was almost more than he could bear. He had never known it could be like this.

Love for her hit him like a falling boulder. It boiled up in him, the heat so intense he came immediately. To his shock and pleasure, she did not pull away, spewing and gagging as he would have expected. Instead she suckled him, draining him of every drop until he could take no more.

He cupped her cheeks in his hands. She was so vulnerable. What must it have cost her to trust him like this, his brave highland lassie?

She ran her hands ups his thighs as she stood, sliding her body up his. Ty dipped his head down to capture her mouth. He slipped his tongue between her lips. He groaned as a possessive yen escaped him. He had never held claim to anything in his life, but this woman was *his*. He had never wanted anything so badly.

"I love that ye taste of me." He swiped his tongue over her swollen lips. He continued to hold her face in his hands as they stumbled to the bed. Kenna's hands were busy removing her clothing. She was completely naked by the time she bumped the back of her knees against the bed frame and fell back upon it with a tinkling laugh. Ty poised over her, his arms locked on either side, and drank in the glorious sight of her perfect body.

He dropped down and caught a nipple between his lips. It hardened into a tight bud against the roof of his mouth. Kenna groaned, sending a jolt of lust straight to his core. He sank into her.

His throat went dry. Ty did not move, ready to explode inside her, his earlier release not nearly enough to satisfy the lust in his heart for this woman, *his* woman.

When he had the turmoil under control, he pulled out of her, thrusting back inside and starting a rhythm that had her moaning and calling out his name. He kissed her, pouring out all the passion he'd been missing in all his long lonely life. As he did, he came with such intensity he thought he would go blind.

Kenna's release exploded around him, draining him. He pulled back and stared at her, savoring the first real happiness he had ever known.

His overwhelming passion spent, he was overcome with fear. How would she react to him now that it was all over? Would she once again have that look of mistrust, that look that waited for him to strike?

Or would she look at him in a way no one ever had before?

With love.

***

Kenna lifted her face to the sun, warm for this time of year. The plod of her horse could easily rock her to sleep if she was not careful. She was tired after the exhaustive night of lovemaking she had shared with Ty.

She smiled a shy smile. She had allowed herself to be brazen, to experience the joy of being with a man who was tender, attentive. Selfless. Her heart soared. She tried to squelch it. She remembered a time when she would have been afraid to touch him, for him to touch her. She asked herself again how he could have changed so much but shrugged off her misgivings. Five years *was* a long time.

She wanted to believe in him. There was so much more to him than the sadistic brute she married or the *cockster* he now pretended to be. He was raw on the inside, vulnerable. What had happened to crush him so deeply? She sensed soul-wrenching loneliness in him and, despite the past, wanted to fill that void. She wanted to comfort the man he had become, to hold him close and show him the love she was capable of if only he would let her.

The idea startled her so much she had to quickly right her seat before she fell from her horse. Could she ever love him? Kenna slid her gaze to where he rode beside her. She had to catch her breath every time she looked at him. He had grown into such a handsome man. Battle scars did not distract from his rugged features but instead gave him a look of manliness that called to everything in her that was female. Silky, strands of his long hair caught the wind and lifted behind him, tendrils of seduction reaching out for her.

Kenna could see beneath those good looks to the man beneath, and thus far, she liked what she saw.

Aye, she could love this man.

Suddenly, Ty stiffened. He slowed his horse, edging closer to her and scanning the hillocks surrounding them. Before Kenna could question him, they were surrounded by a band of men she did not recognize. Her heart fell as a brush of fear skittered up the back of her neck. She was little relieved that the men were clad in Vass colors. She well knew the propensity for violence sported by her husband's clan. She relaxed somewhat when she spotted a woman among them.

"Greetings cousin," one of the men addressed Ty.

Her husband did not return the greeting, but nodded at each of the men in turn. "A few days early for the gatherin', are ye not?"

"Weel, yer father sent us on ahead to get yer sister settled before the others arrive."

Kenna looked at the woman. She recalled her name was Mira, but they had never met. Her slight frame remained stiff as sword. She chewed her bottom lip with relentless assault. She had the same dark hair as Ty and bore a striking resemblance to their father. She kept her eyes downcast but glanced up at Kenna for a heartbeat before looking away again.

Kenna saw anxiety in that brief glance and wondered what torment this wisp of a girl had suffered at the hands of her older brother. It could not have been easy growing up a girl in the Vass household. Mira did not know this new Ty. She would only remember him as the bully he surely had been.

Kenna could well understand Mira's unease. Little more than a girl, she seemed small and insignificant among the men who were there to protect her. And a surly looking lot they were, Ty's clansmen.

Kenna shuddered.

Ty pushed his way through them until his stallion drew up alongside Mira's. He stood up in his stirrups and pressed a kiss just above her brow. Mira's eyes very nearly popped right out of her head.

Kenna would have found the scene touching if not for the realization that everyone else's attention was focused on *her*.

There were eight in all. One of the men spurred his horse to a walk. He did not meet her gaze as he moved around her in a slow arc. Instead he considered her from a distance that did little to make her feel safe. His lecherous grin revealed teeth the color of aged wood.

She jumped when someone else from the group spoke. "I hope the fucking Clearys are no' here yet. If we're t' have a chance in hell -"

The man was quickly shushed with a punch to the shoulder from a nearby comrade and a mumbled, "That's his wife, ye daft bastard."

All eyes turned on her in that instant. The newcomers looked at her with considerably more interest and closed the circle around her.

"She given ye a Cleary bastard yet, Ty? Yer father promised some of us a go once ye had an heir." The man who had been circling her like a hawk over a trapped rabbit drew closer.

Kenna sucked in a sharp breath and looked again to her husband.

Ty gave a quick, disgusted snort and took hold of Mira's horse. "Doona be vulgar. Ye'll not be getting' yer fucking cock anywhere near my wife." He turned and called to the others. "'Tis still an hour's ride to the castle."

He let go of the horse when they reached Kenna. "The two of ye ride on. We'll be right behind."

"But - " Kenna began.

He cut her off with a scathing look. Ty was once again the scowling, frightening man she had married. There was an ugly twist to his mouth she recognized, and resented. He tugged at the sash of his kilt. "Do what I tell ye, Kenna."

She seared him with a equally scathing look before wheeling her horse away and pressing her heels to the mare's flanks.

She surprised herself by her audacity, but disappointment fueled her courage. This entire charade was a ruse to get her to relax her guard. But to what purpose? What were they up to? Was she being over active in her imaginings, or was her husband the ultimate deceiver?

***

They arrived at the castle to find the Clearys already settled. Hackles rose as the warriors of Clan Vass invaded the walls, greeting their new comrades with fake joviality. They were loud, arrogant and genuinely overbearing. The Clearys tossed back seemingly good-natured insults, all the while keeping one hand on the hilt of their swords.

Ty raked a hand through his hair. *What next?* His plan would never work if these unexpected interferences continued to drive him off course.

He looked around for Kenna and spotted her across the room, caught up greeting cousins she likely had not seen in five years or more.

His heart lurched. His plan could not fail. If it did, Clan Vass would rain down destruction on the Clearys, wiping them out with a single blow.

His wife would be devastated.

He could not let that happen. These past days with her had been like nothing he ever expected to experience. He was determined to bring peace to these lands, and win the heart of his wife.

But he was not a fighter. He was a lover. He would have to deter the bitter feud by cunning and charm.

Easily said when all he really wanted to do was slit his *cousin's* throat. The man's vulgarity and insult to Kenna were enough to challenge any man's honor. But the content of that insult instilled within him a vision that sent him into a mind-numbing rage. If he had not removed them from that situation, things could have gone very badly.

Keeping his anger in check had been more difficult than he would have thought. He had never known jealousy, intrinsically aware of the danger in allowing it. He had known people who had gone mad coveting what others had.

But as he watched her, a single avowal engulfed him. Kenna was his. Any man who insinuated otherwise would find himself in a pool of his own blood. Whatever happened, Liam Vass would not live to see another spring.

He swallowed his anxiety and pasted on a smile that could subdue a Hun. "Greetings, brethren, and welcome." When he caught Kenna's eye, he inclined his head toward the door. "I'll leave ye all to spread yer blankets here in the hall." He turned and headed to the family's private rooms. Kenna close on his heels.

As soon as he closed the door, she started on him. "What are you hiding?"

He combed his hair back, again, searching for a cord to bind it. "Nothing," he said, moving objects around in his search. He picked up Kenna's brush, found nothing and dropped it with a frustrated sigh.

Kenna came forward and pulled open a drawer. After riffling through a box inside, she stuck a length of leather between her teeth and reached up to gather the mass of hair behind his neck. Dividing it into three sections, she began plaiting it down his back.

"There is something you are not telling me," she said.

Where do I begin? Ty closed his eyes, silently pleading with her not to ask questions. He could not tell her, not now. She still had that look of mistrust about her. He may have made the hopeful assertion, but she wasn't all his.

Not yet.

Soon, however, she would be. When this gathering was over, his sister betrothed to the laird's son, and Kenna's family safely back home, then he would tell her the truth. He could lie to the world, but not the woman he loved. He would trust his fate to her. He only prayed that she was true.

***

Kenna had no sooner secured the knot at the end of his braid than a ruckus erupted in the hall. Pulling his sword from the sheath at his waist, Ty rushed to the door and yanked it open. She could not keep up as he raced ahead of her.

Skidding to a halt at the entrance to the hall, she cried out at the chaos. She did not want to see what she was seeing. Her insides grew cold as horror gripped her. This couldn't be happening.

Her mother's sister's son lay sprawled not far from her. His sightless eyes stared up at the rafters, his entrails a mass on the rushes beside him. More bodies were strewn around the room, most of them wearing Cleary colors.

She backed away, clutching her stomach and keeping one hand over her mouth to stifle the bile that threatened to overwhelm her. She turned and fled back the way she had come, praying Isla was in her room.

She burst in. Mrs. Dingwell screamed at the sudden intrusion. She hovered in a corner shielding Isla. She came to her feet as soon as she recognized her. Kenna wasted no time. She scooped Isla up into her arms and secreted her away through a door hidden behind a tapestry, Mrs. Dingwell right behind her.

They ran through the darkness, Kenna cradling her daughter and choking back tears. He had betrayed her, lured her family here for slaughter. She swallowed hard. How could she have been such a fool? A person would have to be daft to believe another could change so much.

She coughed on a sob and pushed through the secret door a quarter mile from the castle. They broke out into the shadows of dusk, their escape hidden by the hillocks surrounding Castle Vass. She looked back, pausing at the top of a knoll and hugging Isla tight. She let her tears come freely now, anger turning to disappointment. Nearly a month ago, she had watched him ride over these hills, dreading every heartbeat that brought him closer.

He made her believe he was changed. She believed because she desperately wanted to.

But it was all a ruse. Her dream was shattered. She brushed away her tears. She would not mourn for a lie. She turned and headed for the trees, leaving

Mrs. Dingwell to keep up as best she could. Kenna would try to intercept any other members of her clan before they crossed into Vass lands. Otherwise she and Isla would be all that was left of the Clearys.

CHAPTER FOUR

Kenna sat rigid, unable to escape her surroundings. The atmosphere, ripe with sorrow, erupted occasionally with abrupt calls for vengeance or a sudden wail of despair.

She was in the hall of her grandfather's house at Braemore. It was not Castle Vass, but it was a stronghold of immense authority nonetheless. Surviving members of her family had gathered to mourn the loss of loved ones. In the three days since she had been home, the tension had only grown.

Home. She felt like an outsider even though many had welcomed back into the fold like a lost lamb. A few looked at her with an expression of sympathy, well knowing of Ty Vass' penchant for cruelty.

Others regarded her with profound conviction. Had she not assured them of their safety, by her own hand? Had she allied with her husband then turned sides when it was in her best interest?

She was a Cleary, her daughter was a Cleary. How could anyone believe she was capable of such treachery? It was her grandfather who had been in league with the Munro, who insisted she marry into the Vass family. Was it her fault their plan to unite the clans had failed?

She gritted her teeth, swept by anger, frustration, self-sympathy. It was unfair. She had escaped and made her way back in the darkness with a child and an old woman, all in an effort to warn other members of her family before more lives had been lost. She had likely saved many from the trap that awaited them at Castle Vass. Did that not count for something?

She tried to ignore the accusing stares, but found it nigh impossible. To make matters worse, Gavin had been following at her heels like a hound. Her childhood swain sat next to her now, pretending oblivion each time she pushed his wandering hand from her knee.

"Doona let one unpleasant encounter put ye off love-making, Kenna." He leaned closer, lowering his voice so only she could hear.

Kenna curled her lip, repulsed by the moist feel of his breath on her skin. She almost chuckled at the understatement. *One unpleasant encounter.* Her wedding night had been far beyond unpleasant. Brutal. Horrifying.

She pushed his hand from her knee again and scooted a few inches down the bench. Undeterred, he slid closer. "I have heard the rumors. I know your wedding night could not have been what you dreamed of as an untried maid, a blushing bride. Are the rumors true?"

Kenna swallowed hard. She would not share her suffering, her intimate fears about that horrible night. Especially not with *him*. She shuddered at the memories she was forever trying to block out.

Unlike the reunion she had had with her husband nearly a month ago. Her apprehension over his homecoming had been squelched almost immediately by his attentive gentleness.

Her heart broke. Ty had played her false. It was bad enough he had betrayed her, that he made her believe in a fae tale. But the loss of so many members of her family was unforgivable. She had foolishly opened her heart, even when her mind kept warning her. She had desperately wanted to believe he was a different man, that he was a man who could be loved.

She would never have thought Ty Vass capable of such a performance. He was a simple man, thick-witted even, well-known for his ruthless brutality, his skill with a weapon. He was merciless, selfish, but no one would describe him as being shrewd. Trickery and deception were not his strongest abilities.

He had fooled everyone. Those who lived at the castle had fallen, almost immediately, under his spell. Having suffered the most, Kenna had been more wary, suspicious of his smiling face, his charm and wit. Leastwise in the beginning. But then she too had been drawn into his web of lies.

The now familiar clench of her heart brought tears to her eyes, but she brushed them away. She could only attribute her foolishness to her strong desire to believe. She *wanted* him to be a husband she could love, a man who would protect his people, who could run Castle Vass with authority based on something besides fear.

Gavin droned on next to her. Kenna glanced at him. He was still handsome. Auburn waves framed his face, giving him a boyish look that was hard to resist. She had planned to marry him ever since she was a girl. He had given her her first kiss, on a sunny afternoon of her thirteenth summer. All the girls wanted him, but he had chosen her. Kenna vowed, after that first kiss, that he would be hers one day.

They would have married, too, if Grandfather had not agreed to the Munro's demand for peace. The solution was to combine the two families by marrying Kenna of to the Vass' eldest son.

She leaned forward and looked at her grandfather down the length of table. Would he have made such an agreement if he had known what her wedding night was going to be like? She sat back.

Probably. He loved his family but believed each one of them should be willing to suffer for the good of the clan. He had seen her invitation to the gathering as the well-earned reward for his sacrifice. The two clans, Cleary and the Vass, gathered together to celebrate the union of their family with the Munro clan. Peace was assured. In a few generations, the old hatreds would be forgotten.

Gavin leaned closer, rubbing his wet lips against her ear as he whispered amorous suggestions that made her skin crawl. She pushed to her feet and climbed over the bench, unable to get away from him fast enough.

"Where are you going?"

She wanted to snarl that she owed him no explanation, but she kept her annoyance in check. "'Tis a private matter, Gavin. You will excuse me?" He had that look about him, like he might follow. "Wait for me here. I'll return shortly."

She whirled before he could answer and hefted her skirt. She sensed his intense stare as she hurried from the hall.

***

Kenna stopped in the corridor, her back against the rough stucco covering the stone wall, eyes closed. *Ugh,* she thought. *How could I have ever thought I wanted to marry him?* Now that she had known the true pleasures of the marriage bed, would she ever be able settle for less? She had decided her enjoyment of bedplay was not tied to feelings of love or infatuation. After all, Ty had shown her great pleasure, and she certainly did not love him.

Her eyes snapped open. Did she? After five years of profound hatred, could she have fallen in love with her husband in so short a time? Had he consigned her to the ultimate penance? Her broken heart sank as she realized the truth. She told herself she did not love Ty Vass. She had fallen for the dream he had become, the imposter who had taken his place.

Again that nagging doubt tickled the back of her neck. *He was a different man.* But how different?

If the man now occupying Ty's place as laird of Castle Vass was not actually Ty Vass, who was he and what did he want? She thought back to the day of the attack. When they had encountered his brethren, he had become tense, alert. He had done nothing whatsoever to defend her honor, but he could hardly have been expected to fight eight burly highlanders single-handedly.

Instead he had played it smart, maneuvering his wife and sister out of harm's way while maintaining his ruse. She tried to remember seeing him in the hall during the fight. She had been so horrified by the carnage, she could not remember seeing him at all. Had he helped slaughter her family? Or had he been trying to control the chaos?

If he is not Ty, who is he? she wondered again. A distant relative, perhaps? Their uncanny resemblance would make it plausible, but his appearance *had* changed. The patch over his eye hid most of his face, so it was difficult to discern his features. His boots did not fit. He was more solid, muscular, but that could have come from so many years fighting on the battlefield. Then there was the size of his...

Heat rushed to her face. Kenna glanced around, relieved that she was alone. Taking a deep breath, she allowed herself to remember his...his...man part. A secret smile touched her lips. The very image sent waves of desire to her core. She let her head fall back against the wall and ground her thighs together.

He had been so gentle, so patient with her. Most times, leastwise. Other times he had seemed a man possessed, but in a good way. He had wanted *her*. The pleasure he took then was forceful, vigorous but never at the expense of her own enjoyment. Thy Ty Vass she remembered from the early days of her marriage would have prevented her enjoyment at all costs.

More proof that he was not who he said he was.

She needed to find out and to do that, she would have to go back. But how? And what about Isla? The trek here had been harrowing, to say the least. She would not take her daughter out into the wilds of the highlands without an escort, not again, not unless there was no other choice.

Kenna had brought that choice with her. Mrs. Dingwell.

Determined to find the house keeper and come up with a plan, she pushed away from the wall...right into the arms of her childhood suitor.

Gavin caught her against him, holding firm when she squirmed in his arms. "Shh, shh. Relax, Kenna. 'Tis only me."

She stopped squirming and stood rigid in his embrace. "Let go of me, Gavin."

Instead, he squeezed her tighter. "But feel, Kenna." He ground his hips against her, mumbling into her hair. "Feel how badly I want you. I will never hurt you. I can show you pleasure you only dreamed about."

I seriously doubt that, she thought. His firm hold was not threatening. But Kenna rose to a panic, nonetheless. Memories of the vile acts she had been forced to perform after her wedding came rushing back. By the time Gavin forced his mouth on hers, she was nearly fit to be tied.

She began to fight in earnest now, so much so, Gavin let go of her immediately. The sudden release caused her to lose her balance. If he had not caught her arm, she would have hit the floor like a stone.

He held her in a firm grip, his frustrated expression barely visible in the dim light of the corridor. She snatched her arm from his grasp. "Unhand me," she snarled.

"What is wrong with you? I remember a time when you would sneak out to meet me behind the stables to share a kiss. An' ye were but a wee lassie then."

"No more, Gavin. I am a married woman now." Not that it would have made any difference. Gavin's kisses did not thrill her the way they had done when they were youngsters. Nothing was the same as she remembered. She had been home for three days, and she felt more like an outsider every day.

Gavin rested one hand on the wall next her head and leaned in with a conspiratorial whisper. "Not for long, sweeting. Let me help you forget your brute of a husband." He bent down and pressed his moist lips to her throat.

Nothing happened.

No smattering of gooseflesh pricked her skin. No wild racing affected her heart. She had no desire to get naked as soon as possible.

Kenna stepped away from him, putting as much distance between them as she could in the narrow confines. "No, Gavin. I am sorry, but..."

His sweet countenance changed instantly. Anger clouded his features as he advanced on her. "You spread your legs for that worm, yet ye'll not welcome the embrace of yer own kinsman?"

Kenna's mouth dropped open. The rage on his face would have frightened her into silence in the past, but she had learned a few things as the wife of Ty Vass. She fixed him with an angry look of her own. "You watch your vulgar mouth with me, Gavin Mackintosh, or I will tell your mother."

His moist lips spread into a wicked grin. "Go ahead. I'm no longer a boyling afraid of his mother." He grabbed her arms and pulled her so hard against him, she could not breathe for a moment. He crushed his mouth down on hers in a painful kiss, pushing his tongue against her tightly pressed lips in a vicious effort to invade her.

When she could breathe again, her head cleared. Without further thought, she brought her knee up to his groin with as much force as she could muster.

Gavin released her and doubled over in pain. He clutched himself with one hand and reached to support himself against the wall with the other.

"I hear she still takes a switch to your backside when you need it."

He shook his head, barely able to speak. "No, no please. Doona tell her. 'Twon't happen again, Kenna. I promise."

She thought to say more, but decided against it. He was not worth it. Besides, she had more important things to think about. Without another word, she turned on her heel and headed back to the hall.

When she arrived, she found everyone present on their feet, goblets raised. Her grandfather stood on the dais, looking out over his clansmen, his own goblet raised.

"To the all-out destruction of Clan Vass!" Despite his age, his voice carried, strong and determined.

The room exploded into shouts of agreement as half of her family vowed to destroy the other half.

***

Kenna slipped back out the way she had entered and scurried to the stairs. She climbed up to the room she shared with Isla and Mrs. Dingwell, pushed inside and closed the door behind her. Isla lay buried in the bedclothes, sound asleep in the middle of the bed. Mrs. Dingwell jabbed a piece of cloth with a needle by the faint light of a candle.

She looked up when Kenna entered. "Ah, there ye are, missus.

"You didn't have wait up for me," Kenna pointed out. "Ye'll go blind trying to work with so little light."

Mrs. Dingwell picked up the candle and held it slightly over head while she studied her. She gasped and set her sewing aside. "Are ye all right, then?"

Kenna shook her head, fighting back tears.

Mrs. Dingwell set the candle down as well and crossed the room to her. "There now, dear. What's happened t'get ye so upset?"

Kenna let the housekeeper lead her over to the bed where she sat down with a huff. "They are going to kill each other."

Mrs. Dingwell fetched a cup of water. "Who?" she asked handing Kenna the cup.

"All of them," Kenna fairly wailed in despair. She waved her hand obscurely towards the door. The Clearys. The Vass'. They willna stop until everyone is dead."

Mrs. Dingwell pressed her lips into a tight line and nodded. "Aye, I fear ye're right." She returned to her seat and took up her sewing again. "Although, I doona think the laird had anything to do with the attack on the Clearys."

Kenna sat up taller. "The laird? You mean Ty?"

"Who else? I daresay Laird Vass is a changed man since his ordeal in France. Have ye not noticed?"

Kenna scrubbed her face with both hands. "Have I? My brain is all a-fuddle trying to figure him out. I assumed it was all a ruse to lure the Clearys to Castle Vass."

Mrs. Dingwell shook her head. "Ty Vass is not so great an actor to pull off such a performance. No. I suspect his father is behind it."

"His father?" Kenna had nearly forgotten that her good-father had paid a visit the same day Ty returned from France. What had they talked about? Had they devised the plan knowing the Clearys would attend a gathering on behalf of Clan Mackintosh? "But Ty would do whatever his father said," Kenna argued.

"The old Ty, perhaps." She looked up from her needlework. "I was in the hall when the attack started. I ran for the bairn's room as fast as I could, but I saw the laird amidst the chaos. He was trying to break up the fighting." She looked back down at her sewing. "Or so it seemed."

Kenna tried to recall the scene that day. She had only lingered for a moment, not enough time to determine anyone's motives. She did not remember seeing Ty, but recalled how he had tried to protect her and Mira that day on the way back from the cottage.

Could Mrs. Dingwell be right? She was afraid to let such hope into her heart. She couldn't bear such disappointment again. But she did want to believe.

She loved him. She knew that now, and more than anything, she wanted to believe he was changed. He had to be an imposter, for she could never have loved her husband the way she did this man.

More and more of their conversations came back to her, words whispered in the dark of night, in the privacy of their bed chamber. It slowly dawned on her that he cared for her, too. If only he had trusted her that day at the cottage, or afterwards when they had escorted his clansmen back to Castle Vass. He could have told her his secrets then. So much sorrow and resentment could have been avoided if he had told her the truth. He wanted the same thing she did.

Peace. They could have worked together somehow to prevent the tragedy of that day.

Kenna shot to her feet and began gathering up what few provision were on hand. She would not make the same mistake he had. She would trust him. And she would not wait too long to do so, either.

She was going now.

***

About halfway between midnight and daybreak, Kenna slipped from her grandfather's house. She dropped the sack she carried at the stable door and stepped inside. When she left to be married, she had been forced to leave her beloved gelding behind. Well, not this time.

She made her way down the stalls until she came to his. He lifted his head at her sudden appearance from the darkness, but showed no other reaction. She opened the gate and went in. "Have you forgotten me, Rahm?" She scratched him at the top of his shoulders, just where his thick mane ended. He actually arched his back, making her laugh and dig her nails in that much harder.

With a final pat, she went back out into the center aisle and gathered his tack. It only took a few moments to get him ready. When she was done, she led him back out and gathered her supplies. She mounted in one swift movement and nudged him toward the gate.

The last time she had made this trek, she had been on her way to take part in a marriage she dreaded with her entire soul. Uncertainty brought on similar emotions, but this time, she had higher hopes. This time, she knew the man she was going to meet was gentle and loving. She would not consider that she could be wrong about him. She couldn't be.

But caution dictated she take no chances with her daughter, so she had left her in Mrs. Dingwell's care.

Both of them would be perfectly safe here at her grandfather's house. Of that she was sure.

Her plan was to visit Laird Munro, to seek his assistance in calming her feuding family and bring Ty's over-ambitious father to heel.

That was a meeting she dreaded. Why would the powerful leader of such a large clan listen to her? She was nothing more than a woman, a pawn to be used for men's games, war games or love games made little difference.

She needed courage, and there was only one place to get it.

***

Kenna caught sight of her cottage just before nightfall of the following day. As she approached, she circled the mound, surveying the ground and peering into the brambles. She was not looking for the entrance. She knew this place better than any other. But there was something else, something that made the tiny hairs on her neck stand up.

Someone had been here. She was sure of it, even though she could see no ready evidence. She sat on her horse for a while, listening to the sounds of chirping birds, the babble of a nearby creek, twittering insects. But she detected no other sound that would alert her to danger. So, removing her knife from her belt and holding it at the ready, she dismounted and pushed the door open just enough to squeeze inside.

She screamed when a pair of beefy arms entrapped her. She fought like a banshee, having sworn to die before allowing anyone to ever again do her bodily harm.

"Shh…shh. 'Tis me, *a ghrá.*"

Her captor's thick brogue finally began to seep through her fog of terror. Kenna ceased her struggle, realizing it was Ty who held her in such a strong, inescapable embrace.

"Ty?" Kenna wrapped her arms around his waist, resting her cheek on the hard mound of his chest. He held her with such gentle affection, any doubt about his identity fled.

She pulled back and pushed up to her tiptoes to plant a kiss on his lips. After a lingering moment of sheer bliss, she stepped away. She gasped. His eye patch was gone, leaving his face uncovered and almost too handsome to look at. Two clear eyes, vibrant as lush foliage, stared back at her.

"You are not Ty Vass," she said in a quiet voice. He did not deny it. He said nothing at all, just stood before her, accused and awaiting sentence. "Who are ye, then?"

With a resigned hobble, he crossed to the table and drank from a goblet sitting there. He looked back at her with both eyes. "My true name is Ian," he said in a voice so low, she had to strain to hear it.

"Where is my husband?"

He took a deep breath and let it out slowly. "He was killed in battle."

Kenna refused to smile, for surely she would burn in Hell for such wickedness. But she made no effort to hide her relief. "Does anyone else know?"

He shook his head. "You alone, *a ghrá*."

Now Kenna did smile. She broke into a huge grin and flung herself at him. He caught her in his arms and kissed her with the hunger of a starving man. Kenna pulled back to catch her breath. She cupped his face in both hands, her eyes darting back and forth between his. "I love you, Ian."

He responded by placing one finger over her lips. "From this moment on, you can never call me that. Ian of no familial name no longer exists. I am Ty Vass and will remain so until the end of my days."

Kenna swallowed hard and nodded. "Our secret," she whispered. "Who are ye? Who is your family?"

"You are my family, Kenna. You and Isla. Together we will make this work. We will bring peace to these lands." He kissed her again, a bone-deep kiss full of promise and love. He lifted her into his arms, cradling her against his chest, and carried her to the bed without taking his mouth from hers. He laid her down gently and removed his clothes.

Kenna grinned up at him as he stripped naked. He was like one of the old gods, powerful, strong.

He dropped down on top of her, supporting his mass with hands either side of her head, elbows braced. He dropped his head between his shoulders, capturing her bottom lip between his teeth.

Kenna clasped his backside in both hands. Gooseflesh tickled her palms, and she marveled that she could have such an effect on so potent a man.

His kiss was intoxicating, so when he pulled away, she groaned with disappointment.

He smiled down at her, his face hidden now in shadow. "Tomorrow, *a ghrá*," he whispered. "Tomorrow we will save the world. Tonight is ours."

THE END

Gods of the Highlands

Other Books by Bambi Lynn

Bambi Lynn

Bambi Lynn graduated from the University of Maryland European Division with bachelor's degrees in English and History. She writes Historical [and Contemporary] Paranormal Romances set in Scotland.

What kind of Paranormal? Vampires? Werewolves? Ghosts? Her stories feature Celtic demi-gods, Highlanders with powers beyond mere humans, lost souls whose only salvation is the love of the right woman.

Connect with Bambi online:
http://www.bambilynn.net
http://www.facebook.com/BambiLynn.HotHistoricals
http://www.twitter.com/hot_historicals

REMEMBERING SKYLINE

Skyline Mountain Book 3

by

LESIA FLYNN

Lesia Flynn

Skyline Mountain
Where seasons change, love reigns, and there's plenty of fun for all.

This Valentine's Day could last forever. . .

BENJAMIN MURRAY has it all—land, business, and all of the adventure his heart desires. After an accident leaves him without memory of who he was before, Ben mistakenly assumes he's Scottish and sets off on a highland charade to reclaim his identity. But can his forgotten childhood sweetheart be persuaded by his newly acquired sexy swagger?

CASSIDY SPENCER has had enough and Benjamin Murray is at the top of her list! All she wants is a post-Christmas getaway to revise her happily-ever-after plan, one without Ben and his lack of interest. But before she can hightail it out of town, life takes an unexpected turn. Now she can't get away from Ben or his affections, and he doesn't even know his own name.

Lesia Flynn

For Angela and Mac

REMEMBERING SKYLINE

Acknowledgments

A while back I found myself in a pickle. I had to make a quick trip to the grocery store and the only means of transportation was in the truck my friends Angela and Mac rented while visiting me. When I tried to climb into the truck, it became clear that I needed some assistance. I did what any other short person would do, I retrieved my household stepstool! Imagine the surprise when I had to step down (and back up again after shopping) into the parking lot in front of my small town onlookers. Mac made a ceremonious show of it calling on her most well-mannered royal behavior. It was one of those moments none of us had a camera for and one we will never forget. This was the occasion that inspired a Dodge Ram in Ben and Cassidy's story. It was hilarious fun, much like any time the three of us are together! Thank you Angela and Mac! Without you, life would be boring and likely much more hazardous for me.

And sometimes, life surprises you with the people that walk into your life. Bambi Lynn and Amy Boyles are just that, a very welcome surprise! These ladies came into my life and amazed me with their commitment, patience, and oftentimes, their laughter. Thank you both for the opportunity to work together. You ladies amaze me!

Two other women who have made an incredible difference are my editors, Betty Bolté and C.E.

Lesia Flynn

Irwin. Thank you, ladies, for catching my hiccups and mistakes and helping polish this story.

Most importantly, thank you to my readers! Your willingness to purchase and read my books is humbling. I appreciate each and every one of you. You are a vital part of my dream come true.

Finally, my love and appreciation to my family for never tiring of my zany, crazy antics. I appreciate and thank you all, even the beloved Chali2Na, our tuxedo wearing, resident guardian cat.

CHAPTER ONE

IT WAS LIKE the first time she'd laid eyes on him. The sun glistened off his back making him appear like a fabled demigod. His muscles rippled and caused her brain to short-circuit enough to hear a mysterious Bedouin song playing inside her mind, reeling her in with its rhythmic trance of lust. And it was lust. Pure unadulterated lust that made her breathe in deeply and then exhale with sheer appreciation of the man. Even knowing it was lust, Cassidy Spencer stood on the curb of 214 Loveless Lane cemented to the sidewalk watching the man she'd wanted for more years than not as he stripped the final lights from the high gabled roofline, no shirt required, even in the cold of January. Well, it wasn't that cold at sixty-two degrees on an unusually warm, sunny winter's day in Northern Alabama. But still, it was January. He ought to be shot for tempting her hormones up there half naked as he was.

Cassidy pulled herself together, remembered the packed bags sitting in her car parked in the driveway, and forged forward with her agenda fueling her every step. The sooner she got this over with, the sooner she would be on the road to a much needed getaway for one. This Christmas season had beaten her and left her bare. She needed to have a sit-down with herself concerning the state of affairs of her love life. Or lack of love life. There was no better way for that to happen than to get away from the mountain and her people to some place all alone. To think. To plan. To initiate a new year, a new life. A life clearly *without* Ben Murray and the ridiculous ways he clung to that his grandfather had drilled into him regarding the business of life. The elder Murray, God rest his soul, departed this earth over four years ago. There had been plenty of time since then for Ben to adjust his own thinking, to make changes, to be his own man. Clearly, if she was to have a life filled with love and a family of her own, she was the one who would have to change direction. Ben was never going to regard her as anything more than a business manager and friend.

As she reached the bottom of the ladder Ben was using, Dicker came flying around the corner of the house scaring the bejesus out of her with his top volume orders.

"Stop right there and bring yourself down off that ladder, Mr. Murray! You are *not* authorized to take my lights down!" Dicker stopped and slammed both hands onto his hips as he looked up to the top of the ladder. The sight of him made Cassidy smile. His fun-sized body appeared exaggeratedly toppled backwards while the port of his belly greeted the sky. He looked like a cartoon character.

Ben audibly sighed and looked over his shoulder down at the other man. "Dicker, we went through this last year, man. Give it up." He returned his attention to the task of removing lights, essentially ignoring Dicker.

Dicker sputtered as he stepped back a few yards to gain a better hollering angle. "The Homeowners' Association bylaws say. . ."

"I know what they say, Dicker. And this is not negotiable. The Skyline Fire Marshall overrides your rules."

"Dad blasted man! My lights are in impeccable condition. There is no need to examine them! That man only wants to shut me down for next year."

Cassidy watched Dicker as his face rapidly changed from pink to a red glow. He was mad and growing madder by the second. "Umm. Mr. Dickerson?"

Dicker spun on her so fast the grass kicked out behind him. "Don't you start in on me, little missy. And the name's Dicker. Get with the program, will you?" He snarled and turned back to sky-high Ben. "You come down off that ladder this instant boy or I'll pull you off of there myself!"

"No can do, Dicker." Ben spoke calmly over his shoulder again and smiled. "I have one last strand to wind up and I'm done. If you've got an issue with this job you can take it up with the Fire Marshall. I'm only doing what he assigned me to do as a volunteer."

Ben wrapped the cord of lights he was working on, then added them to a hook on his belt. Simultaneously, as he started his descent to the earth, Dicker took off at a full bull run and kicked the extension ladder with all his might.

Cassidy watched in disbelief from another universe as the next ten-hour-long seconds played out. Realization hit Dicker the moment his foot left the metal rails of the ladder. It was as if that ladder, with Ben no more than three rungs from the top, was connected to a puppet string somewhere high in the sky, peeling both man and metal towards the ground in a slow motion scene of horror for all to witness. The air stuck in Cassidy's lungs and paralyzed her whole body long enough for her to see Ben turn his face to hers in shock and terror. She took off at a run, to what she didn't know. Dicker visibly wilted as he prayed out loud to God for his sins and frailties. Ben wrestled to turn his body, grasped the forty-eight-foot extension ladder with his hands behind him readying for the inevitable landing. Someone from the street slammed on their brakes and started screaming. Cassidy turned and saw Jon Frazier's truck angled in the road so as to stop the ladder from hitting the concrete, hopefully placing Ben in the yard across the way. As Ben's fall accelerated, his legs dangled from the ladder downward into the air powered by gravity. Jon positioned himself as close as possible to Ben's destination so as to call on apparent emergency skills. Cassidy changed direction and took off running alongside the ladder, telling herself with every step, *He's going to be okay. We've got this. He's going to be okay. He's going to be okay.*

As if professionally choreographed, metal scraped and groaned as the ladder hit the roof of Jon's truck, levering Ben towards the ground. Nearing the hard dormant surface of the wheat colored grass, Ben reflexively reached out a hand, followed it with the other, and then slammed hard into the ground. He groaned. A collective sigh was heard from the others as the ladder popped back from releasing its occupant. Ben exhaled his relief as he rested on hands and knees. Jon took a step toward him to check for injuries but before he could reach his friend, who had barely leaned back on his haunches, the ladder came down a second time with all its might and slammed Ben in the head, forcing him to the ground with a loud thud. Cassidy screamed. Dicker grasped his heart and began stumbling around, shaking his head in denial of cause and effect. Jon hopped to it, lifted the ladder from Ben's head, and began checking for a pulse as he yelled "Call 911! NOW!"

***

Dings and beep-beep-beeps bounced off the cavernous walls of the emergency room. Cassidy positioned herself in full view of the double doors that divided her from where Ben's caregivers investigated his condition. Her fingers ached from digging into the hard molded chair, but she ignored her own discomfort, staying on point and watching as Jon filled Bear in on the details. While her mind wanted her to throw up, her body didn't remember how. She felt cold and disconnected. Jon, Ben, and Bear had been friends practically their whole lives. It served reason that Bear would be there. They were like brothers, the three of them.

Mama Paula, Bear's mother, who everyone around town counted as their own mother, pushed through double doors wearing her volunteer uniform and sat down next to Cassidy. She pulled Cassidy into her arms and cooed. "I hear you've had a rough day, sugar."

Cassidy let her head fall onto the elder woman's shoulder. "Has it only been one day?"

They sat there for who knows how long with Bear and Jon taking turns pacing and occasionally asking a question of the other. Each time someone came through the interior doors, they all stiffened, waiting for the staff member who appeared to call one of their names.

After a while, a doctor came through to ask for the family of one *Mr. Dickerson.*

Jon rolled his eyes.

Bear growled.

Mama Paula called Dicker an idiot.

Cassidy watched the room to see who, if anyone, came forward. Her heart sank at the lack of response. Even someone as curmudgeonly as Dicker deserved a loved one. Of course, they probably didn't deserve him, no one did. But still.

The doctor checked his clipboard and then called the name out a second time, louder as he scanned the room for any sign of movement.

A petite woman with hair the color of the sun at its highest point in the sky emerged quietly from around the corner of the waiting room. Her eyes held unwaveringly on the doctor with the clipboard as she slowly moved toward him. A young man followed closely behind her, talking too loudly on a cell phone, saying something about an account that he couldn't afford to lose and that he had no choice in the matter of being at the hospital. When he recognized everyone in the smaller waiting area was watching him closely, he reluctantly added, "It's my father." He held everyone's rapt attention then. Before closing the call, he added tightly, "I'll be in touch," and slipped the phone into his trouser pocket.

Curiosity got the best of Cassidy's attention. She stretched her ears in the direction of the new arrivals on the scene. She leaned in and whispered to Mama Paula. "I didn't think Dicker had a family. Did you?"

"Nope." Mama Paula drew that one syllable word out and then up high like a whistle at the end. She sat tall and straight and crossed her arms tight across her chest. One short leg went quickly over the other and her foot began bouncing to the beat of I've-got-to-hear-*THIS*-story! She didn't bother leaning forward. She simply waited. Everybody knew she possessed incredible bionic-mama-hearing.

Cassidy leaned in, bracing herself on her knees to hear every word.

Bear and Jon stood at a safe distance, but they too were zeroed in on the conversation taking place.

The younger man reached out a hand to greet the attending doctor. "I'm Mr. Dickerson's son." He placed a hand on the woman's shoulder and gently urged her forward. "This is my mother, Mrs. Dickerson."

The doctor nodded his greeting. "Perhaps you could help settle Mr. Dickerson so we can take some tests. He's a little," the doctor reached up and smoothed an invisible mustache, "shall we say, high-strung?"

This elicited a round of nodding heads and various mumblings from everyone looking on.

Concern washed over the woman's features. "Is he going to be okay, doctor?"

"Actually, I think he's healthy as a newborn babe. But, since he's insisting he had a heart attack, I have to run a few tests. It's mainly for our peace of mind." He winked at her and smiled." You do understand, right?"

Mrs. Dickerson's shoulders relaxed as she agreed. "I understand he's probably acting a fool, as usual." She moved to make eye contact with lead-heckler-Mama Paula and sighed.

Mama Paula shook her head and turned away.

Dicker's son piped up, taking charge. "Well then, let's get this over with. Lead the way and we'll make him cooperate."

As Dicker's family wound their way to the great inside, the double doors once again swung open, releasing a man from its clutches whose hair had long ago disappeared save for the reach-out-and-touch-someone eyebrows the color of smoke. His shoulders slumped, from years of chart reading no doubt. A foggy haze bathed his eyes in muck that surely he could not see past. Words croaked from his mouth undiscernible. He cleared his throat, covered his mouth with the boney back side of his hand, coughed, and offered a do over with more gusto. "I've got a Mr. Murray in here. Says he has no family." He drew in another fortifying breath. "Anyone want to claim him?"

Before Cassidy could shout out "Yes!" Ben swaggered through the doors, stopped at the doctor's side, snatched the pen out of the doctor's hand, and scratched what could only be guessed as his signature. Then he did something so alarming, Cassidy fell back into her seat and gasped.

The man actually had the audacity to find her eyes, lift his own lips into a sultry, sexy, how-you-doin' grin. And then he winked at her. Ben. He winked at her, Cassidy Spencer. Ben Murray, the object of the Cassidy Spencer Hormone Society of One, bold facedly, in front of the sun and stars, the moon and the entire universe, winked at her, Cassidy Spencer. *What. The. Hell.* And from there he sauntered to the doors that led outside, threw a hand into the sky and waved his final farewell. He was off and out. Over and done. On his own. Healthy as a newborn babe but clearly out of his frickin' mind.

"Somebody better go watch after that boy. I'm not sure he was officially released." Mama Paula shooed at the men to catch up to Ben. "Y'all go! Cassidy and I will figure out this end. But keep those phones handy. I'll bet we've got us some loose ends to tie up."

And she was off and running, directing and barking like she herself was in charge. Well, who was kidding whom? Mama Paula was always in charge no matter the title or location.

CHAPTER TWO

Cassidy was momentarily glued to her seat trying to take it all in and make sense of Ben's actions. Why would he wink at her? Why would he look at her like that, undressing her and licking her from one end of her body to the other all in point zero zero zero three seconds? And lord have mercy on her sinful, lustful soul, where on God's green pastures did he find that swagger he was sporting? It had her steaming up from the inside out and made her want more of him.

From there a bit of craziness ensued, what with doctors demanding, nurses fussing, and Mama Paula going Mama-Drama on them all. Cassidy couldn't take it anymore. She slipped out to her car, glared at her luggage, made a phone call to cancel her reservations, and then headed to the office. Surely that's where he would go. It's always where he went. Ben the business man. All business. No play. Every hour, every day.

Surprisingly when she arrived at The River Rat Boat Rentals and Cottages office, the doors were locked and showed no sign of Ben. She let herself in, adjusted the thermostat, fluttered around, piddling with this and that to pass the time. She gathered the mail, shredded the junk mail, and made a change to a reservation that came in over the phone.

Finally, she decided to stay where she was to wait it out, let Jon and Bear handle Ben. They were more family to him anyway. Surely, Mama Paula would call when there was news. Sitting down at her desk, she powered up her computer and started playing with her toys. Finance sheets, stocks and bonds, forecasts and whatnot filled the afternoon hours. As the sun began its final slip past the tree line, Cassidy remembered she'd dropped Ben's phone in her bag at the hospital. She retrieved it, looked to see if there were any messages but couldn't maneuver past the home screen without a password. She placed it inside the desk for when Ben regained his memory. Then for the billionth time that afternoon, she checked her own phone. Worry settled in.

No calls.

No texts.

No emails.

***

Ben stood in his bedroom trying to wrap his head around his personal identity crisis. Clearly he'd experienced an accident, but the only thing he could remember was wrapping wires and pondering what it would it be like to allow Cassidy into his life on a more intimate level. Why he couldn't do such a thing was beyond him. She looked good enough to eat. It simply didn't make any sense at all to not let her in.

He shook his head at himself. But then, what did he know? Not a lot. Here he stood in a completely unfamiliar place trying to figure out if he should be alone or attached.

Merely a half-hour ago Bear and Jon found him sauntering down a street near the hospital. Of course, he had no idea where he was going so he'd gladly accepted the ride they offered to his house. And while this location didn't match the address on his driver's license, he went with it, assuming they knew better than he did given the circumstances. They were nice enough guys, he decided, as they chatted along the way. They seemed to know each other very well, tried enveloping him with their talk too, leaving Ben to conclude that they must be good friends, the three of them. Ben hadn't offered any input to their conversation. No, he simply enjoyed the ride and took in the details they offered. He'd been careful to listen and learn what was what, especially since the last thing the ER doctor said to him was that his accident had sparked some sort of temporary memory loss. That worked for Ben since he'd been forced to check his wallet for an ID to learn what his own name was. Thankfully, he remembered enough about the practical things of life to know that he carried a wallet. After that, the doctor had gone all technical on Ben with his terminology and risks and all. That was when Ben decided he'd had enough of his hospital visit. He escaped the first chance he got, wearing a scrub shirt he'd found on his way out of the ER interior.

So here he was now, minus Jon and Bear. They'd had someplace to go once they were convinced by a lot of nodding on Ben's part that he could settle himself into his own cabin without their help. Though, it was really half of a cabin, the backside of the offices of The River Rat Boat Rentals and Cottages. Thankfully, it offered a private entrance so he could avoid whoever's car that was parked at the office. Time to put his mind into gear, to try puzzling out who he really was, beyond the photo and the specs of the person on his license.

The room's windows were framed by a dark stained wood worn with years of opening and closing. A small bureau sat against one wall, its mirror large and proud. There wasn't a thing sitting on top, the drawers neatly pushed in all the way. A rug lay across what looked to be a very old and beautifully maintained hardwood floor. Ben ran a hand through his hair where he was reminded of the knot on his head. Right. A concussion. Pretty big bump on the noggin, too. He let out a sigh as he turned to quietly open the closet door to take stock of his wardrobe and search for clues. A hook hung over the inside of the door, empty but clearly used if the semicircle scraping of wood underneath it was an indicator. It was probably where he hung the tool belt Jon had handed him on his way in from the truck. He retrieved the belt from beside the entry door where he'd placed it and looped it over the closet door's hook. Sure enough, the worn places on the wood matched where the belt's hardware met the leather that held his various hand tools.

Inside the closet a long cord hung from the ceiling to engage the overhead light when pulled. The guts of the inside were pretty sparse. A black suit hung toward the back with a silk tie rolled up and stored in the breast pocket, a dress belt slipped over the hook of the hanger. Funerals, weddings, and such, he figured. The coat pocket held a jewelry box with a tie clasp inside. Between him and the suit hung two white shirts, a couple of black and red plaid flannel shirts, and a smattering of dark colored jeans. A worn-to-softness pair of khaki canvas pants were tucked to the right side, possibly forgotten about. Neatly on the floor sat a shiny pair of black dress shoes and a well-used pair of running shoes with an empty space in between, probably for the work boots he was currently wearing.

What interested Ben most was what hung in the very center of the closet, wrapped in a clear plastic bag, likely a dry cleaning bag, all neat and tidy. A kilt. Huh. What the devil did a man need a kilt for? He retrieved the package from the clothes rod, which on closer examination held more than one hanger, and laid it out on the bed for a closer look. Laying in front of him were three kilts, not one. Each one was made of a red and black plaid with a shiny silver thread woven through the fabric. All three were in impeccable condition, soft and beautiful in craftsmanship. Curious.

Ben went back to the bureau to check its contents. Upon opening the top drawer, he found socks and underwear, all black and neatly organized. The next drawer held t-shirts that were folded and stacked with the skill of a very good launderer or someone who was obsessed with order. At least a dozen shirts in all. He ran a hand across the front stack, flipping them like pages of a book. All were in excellent condition. *Good Lord, he was a neat freak.*

He opened the bottom drawer last. Inside was a bright yellow athletic t-shirt, two pairs of running shorts, a pair of pants with a stripe the same yellow as the t-shirt down the side seam, and two pairs of board shorts. Laying on top of it all was a whistle on a rope. Interesting. But he'd saved the best for last, the small drawers on the top of the piece of furniture that were likely meant for jewelry or keepsakes of some type. He opened the one on the right to find a velvet box. Inside was a diamond ring and matching band. The band was engraved with an infinity symbol. Underneath the inner velvet was another band, this one larger, obviously for a man. Unlike the other, it was not engraved. Was he getting married? Ben scanned his mind but couldn't recall a woman in his life except for the thoughts of Cassidy before the accident. He reflected on seeing her at the hospital. He wouldn't mind having her in his life. She was a looker!

He replaced the rings into their nest and closed them away. In the drawer to the left was a set of keys, each labeled and numbered, RRC 1 through RRC 7, and another one simply labeled

RRCO. An engraved metal tag stated the keyring's purpose, *RRC Spare.* So he really was the man who ran these cabins on the river. Again, he replaced the contents of the drawer. Then he removed the wallet from his back pocket and laid its contents on top of the bureau to examine. A driver's license that said he lived on Skyline Mountain Road. Good man. He was an organ donor. An insurance card for an old truck, liability only. Cheapskate. A Visa debit card for Riverland National Bank. A piece of paper with a name and number scrawled across it and today's date. The name was Catherine. A relative maybe? The number was local. Underneath the name and number were the words, return by six. Weird. He didn't know what to make of that piece of information. There were also a few twenty-dollar bills, an old picture of a school-aged girl with Cassidy Spencer printed on the back in very neat handwriting (though, the e's were backward), and a receipt from Henry's Bar B and Cue for a pulled pork sandwich and a beer. That was it. That was the entire contents of his wallet.

Ben scrubbed a hand across his face, his growth of stubble scratched his palm, versed the air with its sound. He looked around the room before proceeding ahead through the only other visible door. The bathroom. Inside the shower was an inexpensive bottle of shampoo and a bar of soap half used. The medicine cabinet was empty save for a tube of toothpaste, a toothbrush, and a stick of deodorant. A towel hung on the towel rod, fresh and clean. A spare was folded neatly and laid on the tank of the toilet. Ben closed the door to check if there was anything on the back side. Nope. Not even a hook.

Ben didn't know what to make of his life. He leaned over the sink, bracing his arms on the counter to stare into eyes he didn't recognize. They weren't brown. They weren't green. They were eyes the color of in-between, whatever that was. His hair was straight and dark, barely long enough to hang in his eyes and pester him. Peering into the mirror, he spoke out loud, questioning his identity to himself. "Who?" Confusion quickly followed like before, at the hospital, when he had answered questions for the doctor. He'd sounded funny, even to himself. Then *and* now, though the doctor paid no mind to it at all.

Ben cleared his throat and gave it another try. "Who urr. . ." He stopped, quirked an eye at his reflection in response to the "r" sound that rolled off his lips. He straightened himself and, placing his hands on his hips, coughed in preparation for yet another attempt, hoping to get a handle on his deep baritone voice. He shook his head, signaling to himself that he was ready, and pushed his words out into the empty air. "Who arr yeh, Benjamin Murree?"

Ben's mouth dropped open, his jaw hung wide. His mind raced in thought of what he was seeing and hearing. In his own head he sounded like everyone else he'd heard that day, speaking perfectly good and normal English.

Deciding to give it another go, Ben thought of something to say and first tested it inside his mind. *My name is Benjamin Murray.* He cleared his throat, hoping, and gave his mouth another shot to say exactly what he'd thought. Oddly, what came out of his mouth was not at all what he'd imagined. "They ca' me Benjamin Murree."

Ben's eyes grew big as the details combined to form a conclusive idea in his mind. The r's convinced him with their deep embellishment of his name. Mix that together with the kilts, the cheap insurance, and, for all that's holy, comprehension hit him upside his head like the proverbial iron skillet. He threw both hands high in the air in recognition of who he was and pumped his arms in quiet celebration. "A'm a *Scot!*"

Frustration melted away into fascination as he began pacing the small spaces of his home. He tried to wrap his mind around all of it. The Scottish brogue combined with his wallet contents and the surroundings of his home made for a very interesting individual. At some point he simply started talking out loud to himself, trying on his new persona and acquainting himself with *Ben the Scot.* When he'd all but worn a new rut into the wood floors, he stopped pacing. "Wha th' devil am ah t' do *now*?"

He fell onto the bed, crossed his legs at the ankles, and raised his arms to prop his head up in thought. If he was a Scot, and he owned land, then he was a *rich* Scot! Never mind the odd phone number with the name Catherine and its return date and time. He owned kilts and land,

and he was a neat freak and a cheapskate, which was probably how he'd gained his wealth. Or he was simply cheap, and well, that was okay with a Scot, too.

Now that he had a jump-start on his identity, Ben decided it was time to get out and about town where he could learn from the locals more of who he really was. So he freshened up and prepared for an adventure in self-discovery. Then it occurred to him, if he was a Scot with a kilt, maybe there was a dagger or a sword somewhere, too. And off he went to see what he could find.

***

Cassidy could not believe the sight displayed for all the world to see right there in front of her very own eyeballs. Straight ahead, far in the back hall of Henry's, was a loud and randy Scotsman. A likely loud, and randy, and *very drunk* Scotsman. Except she knew this man. He was no Scotsman. He was her first love, her one and only true love from all the way back to elementary school. He was one very confused Benjamin Thomas Murray. Cassidy could not believe the spectacle he was providing for the locals.

She turned her head as Henry came around the bar. He slapped a towel over his shoulder and nodded in her direction. He motioned for her to join him at the bar's end nearest to the door. Laughter bellowed from the far reaches of the pool room. Cassidy shuddered and gave thanks for the place not being any more crowded than it was.

"I'm so glad you're here, Cassidy. I knew you'd come right away." Henry wiped his forehead with the back of his beefy hand. "That boy ain't right, I tell you. He's been drinking and carousing since he stepped into the place late this afternoon." He shook his head, worry crossing his features. "I left messages all around town for Jon and Bear but they haven't returned my calls."

"Henry, what on earth has he done?" She jumped at the sound of a loud "whack" coming from Ben's general direction. Ben used a pool stick to fence against someone she didn't know. "Start at the top and tell me everything." She scooted up onto a bar stool.

"Child, he came in here proud as you please, sporting that kilt, first of all. Started barking orders like he owned the place himself. Then that boy marched right up behind *my* bar, scanned the contents of *my* wall and pulled *my* *only* bottle of The Glenlivet down and took a swig *straight from the bottle*. I swaney, Cass! That boy ain't got a lick of sense right now. He's been taking pulls off that bottle going on two hours. He's lost his ever loving mind, he has." Henry huffed loudly, shook his fist in the air, and inhaled another for round two. "Then! *Then*, I tell you! He proceeded to march back to *my* pool room calling players as he went. *In brogue*, no less! That young man?" Henry pointed at Ben's form again for double emphasis, his eyes bulging beyond their sockets. "That man thinks he's a damn *Scot*! I want him out of here, Cass. *Out!*"

Right on cue to enhance and end Henry's tirade, a pool stick flew through the doorway between the dining room and the pool room, slamming against a chair before rattling to the floor. A man sitting at the piano stopped playing to take stock of the situation. He raised an eyebrow at Henry in question.

Cassidy reached across the bar and patted the elder's hand for assurance. "Thank you for calling me, Henry. Don't you worry. I'll get him out of your hair. Fast!"

"You don't understand, sugar. He's not only drinking and living it up himself, but he's buying rounds for everyone in the house! If I didn't know that was Ben Murray I'd say it was normal. But that's not normal for Ben. You and I *both* know it!"

Another round of laughter broke out, coughing up a man from the bowels of the back room. Ben staggered toward Cassidy sporting a kilt, his work boots, and a tee shirt that clung to every muscle the man owned above his waistline.

Cassidy groaned inside. This was not going to be good. Her gut squeezed. She felt a bit of a flutter of warning inside her stomach. Or was that lust? She couldn't tell which with him looking at her like his next meal, and for the second time that day! Ben continued to swagger her way, his face split wide into a grin. He reached up with one hand to rub the hard rippled planes of his middle. If she didn't know better she would've sworn she heard him growl. Eight feet away from her, someone scooted their chair back, bumping into him walking past. Ben lost his already shaky balance, teetered toward another table, then hit it hard enough that the newly filled pitcher of beer toppled over and spilled directly into a man's lap. The man didn't look one bit happy about it.

Ben grappled with the empty pitcher, offering his apologies to the man. He lifted the pitcher high into the air and boldly stated, "Another round for mah pal!" He stood, wobbled, and dusted himself off. "An' put it oan mah tab, jimmy."

Cassidy gave him a hard stare as she placed her hands on her hips. As she began to speak, Ben caught the attention of onlookers. "She's a bonny lass, isn' she mates?" Ben walked up to her without a speck of remorse, placed a hand around her bottom, and pulled her hard against his body.

Cassidy slapped both hands on his chest and shoved hard.

Ben didn't budge.

"You are out of control, Benjamin Murray. Let me go right this instant!" She pushed at him, trying to get away.

People around began laughing and cheering him on. Henry tried to step in, but Ben pushed him away to slip around Cassidy's neck to whisper something in her ear. She wasn't certain what he said, but it sounded something remotely like a woman named Wilma Makemah, her dreams and the night, or some such. Geesh! What did she know about brogue? It made as much sense as pig Latin to her.

Cassidy was ready to pull out the stops and kick the man in his jewels, but before she could act a familiar voice shouted out Ben's name across the room. Everyone went silent. Bear Grecco marched over to Ben, picked him up by the scruff of his shirt, and set him away from Cassidy. "You owe the lady an apology." He waited for Ben to comply.

Aggravation bounced off of Ben. "Who are yeh tae tell me what tae dae?" He stood taller, ready to fight.

"Oh shush, the both of you!" Cassidy wanted to move Ben out of the public eye lickety-split so they could figure out what the heck was going on. "Henry, send his tab to me at the office. I'll settle up with you." She aimed her attention at Bear. "Let's move it! Get him to my car, will you?"

The crowd jeered their offense. "But you said beer on the house for the rest of the night," someone yelled out.

Cassidy couldn't find the heckler, but she addressed the entire room of customers. "Sorry, y'all. This man has suffered a severe trauma to the head. He can't pay for your drinks for the rest of the night. You're all cut off as of right now."

Ben stumbled around Bear. With a drunken slur almost as heavy as his accent, he said, "Ah d'no' lik' yer wit, lassie."

"Yeah? Well I don't like anything about *you* right at this moment, Ben." She slapped Henry on the shoulder. "I'll take care of that bill as soon as you send it to me and I can get to the bank. In the morning is fine with me. Good enough?"

She waited for him to approve. Henry's head bobbed in agreement. Cassidy slipped an arm around Ben's elbow as Bear pulled his other arm toward the exit. Together the three of them got the hell out of there as fast as Bear could drag them to safety.

The cold front that rolled in earlier that day hit them full force as soon as they exited the building. Bear's phone rang. It was Jon. Bear kept moving them towards their destination. Cassidy couldn't tell what they were discussing on the phone, but she did hear the words "Damn Scot!" loud and clear. Bear crammed Ben into his beater truck before getting behind the wheel himself.

"I'll meet you at the office, Cass. Jon'll be there, too. We've got to figure this out before it gets any worse." With that, he was off.

Cassidy rushed to her own car and pulled up right behind them, anxious to put things in order.

CHAPTER THREE

Cassidy sat next to Ben's side on a collapsible camping stool in the storeroom that separated the offices from his private side of the cabin. The room was equipped with an exit door for loading and unloading supplies, a small kitchenette, in addition to the door leading to Ben's personal rooms, the latter of which was dead bolted from the opposite side for his personal privacy. The room they sat in also housed a cot in case it was ever needed for first aid. Clearly there was never a time more needed than now. Though this particular exploration (one Ben Murray, drunk, concussed, and apparently with loss of his memory) was not one she'd ever dreamed she'd need to rescue and administer aid to. She'd spent the past half hour or more talking Ben down from spinning walls, trying to convince him to sleep off the drunken stupor he had acquired. Ben wasn't playing well with her efforts. He kept rambling on and on about ideas he had that seemed to have little to no connection with each other. At one point she wondered if he wasn't simply enamored with his newly acquired accent. At the moment he was voicing new opinions of women, opinions Cassidy knew for certain he did *not* hold in his real heart and soul.

"You're a bonny lass, Cassidy. Ah like th' way yer eyes shimmer like th' color o' th' sea rippling back and forth from blue to green at night's fall." His face relaxed into a sleepy smile. "You're a bonnie lass, you are!" He extended a hand up to touch her face.

Cassidy felt compromised within herself. She knew full well Ben Murray did *not* have feelings or admirations for her, Cassidy Spencer. He made that clear a very long time ago. To this day it made her sad that he didn't want her.

But he touched her with softness as he whispered once again. "Mak' mah dreams come true t' night, Cassi." His hand slipped silkily down her neck, arm, past her elbow, and across her hand. His touch stilled on hers, long enough for Cassidy to wonder if he'd finally found sleep. Then he moved her hand with his own, slipped it across his stomach, reaching down to place her hand around himself, letting her feel where his thoughts had landed. On her. On them. Together.

Cassidy jumped and fell over her chair backwards trying to get away from him. Lordy but he was mighty big and aroused! In the commotion, she heard Mama Paula ask from the office if everything was alright. Alright? *Alright? Are you kidding me? There was absolutely nothing about this day or night that was all right!* She scooped herself up and squeaked out a response, trying her best not to cause further alarm on the other side of the door. When she set the chair back upright on its three legs, she prepared to give Ben a piece of her mind, whispered of course, only to find him with a smile on his face, a hand proudly upon his privates, a serene snore escaping past his lips.

***

"Boys, I don't have the time or the know-how to take this on." Mama Paula did not appear happy to have been pulled away from her monthly book club. Not so much because of the book but because book club was the heartbeat of what's what in Riverland. And tonight she was supposed to find out who was coming home to stay. Gran Raine had promised to make the announcement over cake and coffee and Mama Paula missed it all, everything past the initial greetings of the night. And for what? For these boys to dump on her? "He named the two of you, one after the other, as his Power of Attorney, not me."

"I understand that, Mama Paula. But I can't do this. I'm barely able to keep up with my own business right now." Jon aimed his head in the direction of where Cassidy was trying to settle Ben close by so she could keep an eye on him for the night. "Besides, he made those choices more than ten years ago. He has a lot more at stake nowadays than what he had then. I'm not even sure I'd know where to start."

Mama Paula directed her attention straight at her own son, commanding without speaking a word.

"I can't do it either." Bear crossed his arms over the wall of his big bad self. "I leave for Italy in two days to teach a class at the University for six weeks. You know that, Mama. And no, I'm not canceling. It's already been rescheduled twice in the past eight months. Besides," he said as he pushed back in his chair letting it rock perilously on two feet, "Julia's never been overseas. She's meeting me there after my class for a spring break vacation." He grinned suggestively and wiggled his eyebrows. "I won't be stateside for ten weeks."

Mama Paula slapped her hand at the air towards Bear and shook her head, completely missing the fact that her boy was leaning back in his chair contrary to all that she'd taught him his whole life long. "Boys, I know this is not a good time." She threw her hands up into the air. "Heck! It's never a good time for an emergency!" She fell back into her chair. "I can't do this because, frankly, I'm not qualified. I don't know a thing about his business *or* his holdings. I'd do more harm than good for that boy and you both know it." She stood and shoved her hands into her trouser pockets, clearly deliberating what to do. A loud sound came from behind the door.

"You alright in there, Cassidy?" Mama Paula spoke to the door.

"I'm fine, thanks," came the weak response.

Mama Paula frowned in question to Cassidy's response before returning her attention back to the business at hand. "Well, I don't know what to do exactly, but like his lawyer said on the phone, if you don't take it on, Jon, then it falls to Bear. And, Bear, if you don't take it on, then you have to find someone who is capable of the task of overseeing all of his affairs. You can't slide this onto someone else's plate haphazardly. You're going to have to find someone who knows his business or is capable of getting up to speed *fast*. Someone trustworthy and honest or you two will have to be up in the big middle of it all, regardless of your own times and needs. That's what you agreed to when he asked you to cover his back."

A door swung open quietly. Cassidy eased into the office. "He's out," she said in response to the questioning eyes. "He's in a dead sleep, happy in his own private dream world."

"Well, his private world just got a bit bigger," Mama Paula complained. "And one of you will have to step up to the plate." She gave them all a hard looksy. "Which one of you can stand up to him and keep his affairs best in order, including those ridiculous miserly standards his grandfather instilled in him?" Her hands were on her hips now, in full drama mode, eyeing each one of them in turn.

Jon stood and invited Cassidy to take her desk chair back. She felt out of place in the midst of this emergency. Ben had never let her closer than arm's length even though they'd known each other longer than they had not. No, he wouldn't approve even now, she was certain of it. But then he wouldn't approve of Mama Paula being mixed up in this mess, either. It had nothing to do with their skills or lack of them but everything to do with their gender. Ben Murray, contrary to his earlier behavior, was not a fan of women in charge or meddling in his personal business. With one exception. Cassidy was his business manager because there simply was no one better at it than her. But then, his grandfather was who hired her, not Ben. She knew Ben's business of the rentals and cottages inside and out, backwards and forwards. The only thing about it she didn't know was how to repair a boat. But that was beside the point.

"I was telling the boys that they're either going to have to muster up and take this responsibility to heart or find someone they can trust to do the job right. What do you think, Cassidy? Do you know anyone who Ben would trust his affairs to other than us?"

As the last words came out of Mama Paula's mouth, Jon and Bear peered at each other. A kind of silent language passed between them and left each of them nodding their understanding before turning to look at Cassidy in unison.

Cassidy's stomach ached at the directive they aimed at her. She felt the floor drop out from underneath her. Darkness shrouded the room around her. Suddenly, the air thinned. Realization slammed into her mind like a tank. They were looking to her as Ben's savior. They were asking her to take this on and run with it. They were making her the bad guy to keep Ben safe. Ben would forever hate her afterwards. If there was to be an afterwards. If he ever regained his memory. Bile bit at the back of her throat. She couldn't breathe. Both of the men in front of her beamed as they recognized her awareness.

Mama Paula jumped out of her chair and squealed. "I have the perfect solution y'all! Let's have Cassidy handle his affairs!"

Cassidy couldn't make her words form or sound them out for anyone to hear. All she could do was tell her head to move, to negate their requests, to turn from side to side.

Mama Paula clapped her hands together in joy.

Horror enveloped Cassidy, clenching her heart in its grip.

Bear let his chair fall back to the floor. "This is perfect, Cass! You already know all of the details concerning the business. Hell, you run the whole thing anyway. Surely you know his personal finances and such, right? It's a piece of cake for you!"

Jon stood, and then stretched his shoulders, showing his relief to have this little dilemma solved.

Mama Paula piped up. "And Cassidy! Sugar pie, this is perfect because you can use those fancy investment skills of yours to make everything even better for Ben. He'll be so proud when he comes back around! You'll see."

"What investment skills?" Worry covered Bear's features. "You play the stocks, Cassidy?"

"It's more than playing the stocks, son. She's a money genius! It's like her thing. Her hobby. She can turn air into gold, she can!"

Jon shook his head and let out a low whistle of concern. "Well, it's going to *take* a genius to sidestep Ben's irrational fear of spending money." He set out pacing the length of the room, jingling keys in his pocket nervously. "Of course, I don't have to tell you that, Cass."

Cassidy sat, her eyes grew wild as fear beat at her insides.

Jon paced back towards Mama Paula. "What about that other little detail?"

"Oh yes, right, son. Doc says we can't tell him anything, either. He'll be better off remembering things on his own, so mum's the word, alrighty?" She made a motion to zip her lips for everyone to agree with her.

"No." Cassidy stood and placed both hands flat on her desk, commanding everyone's attention. "No!" Finally, she could speak, thank the Lord above. "You all can *not* ask me to do this. You know what he thinks about women in charge. I can't, y'all. I can't do this. It's not right. Ben would never forgive me for this." Her eyes searched her spectators for agreement or assurance or understanding. Compassion, at the very least. But all she saw staring back at her was a round of smiles.

Bear gave her a two thumbs up. "You've got this, Cass!"

Jon laughed as he agreed with Bear.

Mama Paula all but did a little dance of cheer for her, front and center.

Cassidy lifted her waste paper basket and proceeded to throw up.

***

The following morning, after waking up in the office's foldout chair, Cassidy quickly did her business before peeking in on Ben in the storeroom. He was still sprawled out on the cot, sawing logs. His kilt lay askew, revealing his strong legs. His t-shirt bunched up in the middle, a hand slipped under it as if he'd been rubbing his belly. Contrary to his brawny body, in sleep, Ben Murray looked like an angel. His lips were pink and soft, his hair fell loosely over his cheeks. Peace washed across his face. She gave herself time to admire his serenity. In sleep he was heavenly and beautiful. In the light of day? Handsome and in control, yes. But tranquil? She couldn't remember a day when Ben wasn't stressed or behaving a bit uptight. He was always in a hurry to move on to the next job.

Well, that wasn't quite true. She could remember when they were very young he'd been laid back and easygoing. But then he'd grown up, filled with unreasonable expectations from his grandfather. He responded by placing a lead barrier between himself and everyone else in the entire world. No one was allowed in. He didn't allow his true self out, either. He was an island of a man living in isolation in the midst of a nest of people who loved and adored him. But it didn't matter. That's how he'd set his stage and he was guarding it like a sentinel.

Cassidy eased into the room. She carefully opened the blinds of the small eastern window. Light flooded in, garnering a protest. Cassidy moved into his field of view, hoping for the old Ben to greet her. "Good morning."

Ben peeked at her through his fingers to keep the light at bay. "Please speak softer, lass."

Cassidy snickered. "I'm sure you feel awful, but it's time to face the day. There's work to be done, Benjamin Murray."

Ben groaned out loud as he turned his back to her.

She laughed quietly. "You can ignore me all you want, but the pipes in Cottage No. 3 need to be rewrapped before the bad weather hits at the end of the week. The Murdocks over on Mason Road called this morning, asking when you'd be by to take down their lights. You promised them they were on the schedule right after Dicker. You finished with Dicker yesterday, if you'll recall."

Ben rolled over to face Cassidy. He lifted himself slowly to a sitting position and groaned. "I'll get tae them as soon as somebo'y makes th' hammerin' in mah haed stop a'poundin'." He held his head gingerly, between his knees, breathing in deep and exhaling slowly. "But ah dae nae recall anyone by th' name o' Murdock."

"Yes, well you probably dae nae recall," she said mockingly, "that you don't drink alcohol either." She stared at him hard. "Ever."

Ben didn't look up. He simply moaned in her direction.

She offered a hand. "Come on, big boy. You go to your room and get cleaned up. I'll find you something for the pain along with some food to give you energy for the morning."

CHAPTER FOUR

Ben found Cassidy true to her word. Upon returning to the office after a shower, she'd poured a beastly concoction down his throat, then fed and medicated him. For the most part, he felt better. It didn't hurt that she watched him throughout the meal with concern on her face. He liked her face. Come to think of it, he liked all of her other parts, too. Especially the parts that swayed when she walked away from him, tempting him to reach out and pull her back against him. He couldn't figure out why it was that she always broke free from his grasp, though. Especially since he recalled she'd been fond of him since grade school, loved him even, if he remembered correctly. But she sure was behaving strangely since he left the hospital yesterday, running away from him when he stepped too close. Twice now she'd run scared from his affections. He decided he would be better equipped to tussle with her later, after the day's work was done and he felt more renewed.

But the day had not gone so smoothly, what with the Murdock girls following him around. They tried to sneak a peek underneath his kilt, saying strange things before giggling behind their hands like a couple of pests. Mr. Murdock would do well to lock them in the cooler if he knew what was best for them. On his way back to the office, his truck coughed, sputtered, and then died on the side of the road. He saw no choice but to leave it behind and put one foot in front of the other.

As he walked, Ben considered a few details that pushed at his mind. He understood he was void of his identity, but why did he know how to drive a truck? How was it he hid the knowledge of plumbing inside his mind, but not the details of his family and upbringing, his friends? Where was the reasoning behind what he remembered and what he did not? And another thing, why was Cassie acting like he had the plague every time he went to touch her? As he'd left breakfast that morning, he'd reached over to kiss her cheek. She'd once again taken off running for a task "she'd forgotten."

He set the thoughts aside, focusing on the road and countryside around him. Did he grow up here? Nothing, not the cows on the hills or the river that ran alongside the road, incited any meaning whatsoever in his brain cells. The only solid memory he retained was the sense of affection from Cassie, but then that wasn't really a solid memory if her current actions were any indication. He *did* recognize a sign up ahead that hung dangerously sideways as if its days were numbered, though. But then it might be because he could read the sign, not actually remember the place. The sign read *Knights Garage*. Cars upon rows of cars lined the entrance underneath its faded colors. Surely, someone could help him repair his truck, get him back on the road.

Ben marched up the metal strewn drive and then through the office doors. He slapped a hand down on the counter good naturedly. "G'aftarenoon, Jimmy!"

The man, in a blue work shirt with the name "Charlie" embroidered in red, grunted without looking up at Ben from behind the counter.

"Mah truck seems t' ha' broken down an' needs a bit o' repair." He leaned over the counter to capture the man's attention. "Kin y' help me ou', mah frien'?" Ben let a smile lace his words, hoping to charm the man's attention.

"*Help* is it?" Charlie Knight stood at his full height, a hair above five and a half feet tall. He wrapped his arms around his midsection and crossed them. A voice on the radio behind him announced the time and launched a new song into play before Charlie spoke again. "The name's Charlie. Charlie Knight. Not Jimmy, as you well know. Are you asking *me* for a bit of help with that rat-trap of a truck of yours, Benjamin Murray?"

"Aye, Ah believe A'am." Ben's optimism shone as bright as the sun on a warm summer's day in July.

Charlie turned his back to Ben to rumble around in something out of Ben's sight. Then he changed direction and charged himself around the corner of the counter, dressed in fury and wielding a Billy club in his fist.

Ben took off running, alarm fueling each step he took. Charlie came after him as fast as his body would propel him forward, yelling ugly words about payments denied and work not meeting standards. Ben picked up speed. Halfway down the entrance driveway, a dog caught up to him, barking and nipping at his skirt tails, trying to secure a piece of the kilt firmly into his mouth. Ben stopped and wrestled with the dog, all the while keeping an eye on Charlie Knight gaining on him. It wouldn't do to be unwrapped by a dog and beaten by a crazy mechanic after abandoning his truck on the side of the road, and all in the matter of a few morning hours. Where was his gentle Cassidy to take charge of the situation?

With only seconds to spare, Ben ripped the kilt away from the dog's mouth and took off at a full run. He heard a scuffle behind him. The dog yelped before Charlie let out a line of expletives only a convict would shout. Ben dared to look back around to see the man sprawled across the top of his guard dog in the dirt, with Charlie shaking his weapon in the wind at Ben.

With a chunk of fabric out of his hide, Ben continued to run until he reached the town limits. He checked to see if his phone would make a call. Before he could dial, Cassidy pulled up alongside of him.

"Get in!"

Never before had he been so glad to see someone, anyone, especially his girl with eyes full of kindness.

"You look like hell." Cassidy didn't give him time to buckle up before pulling away from the curb.

"Ah was attacked by a dug."

Cassidy quirked an eyebrow in question. "What's a 'dug'?"

Ben secured his seatbelt then dropped his head back on the headrest and sighed. He rubbed a hand over his heart in attempt to make it slow down. "'Twas th' beast wi' Charlie Knight."

Cassidy slammed on the brakes without warning. The sudden stop pitched Ben forward, painfully engaging his seat belt into action, binding him tightly to the seat.

"Bugger, Lass! Wha''re ye tryin' t' d' t' me, murder?" Ben's eyes jutted out at her.

Cassidy shot her big eyes right back at him. "Tell me," she ground out, "you did *not* go to Knight's Garage for help with your truck, did you?" She waited.

A car drove past, the driver aiming a familiar hand gesture at her. He honked the horn while mouthing something behind the closed windows that clearly was not nice. Cassidy ignored the passerby while waiting for Ben's response.

Ben was confused. His head hurt again now that the medicine was out of his system. He twisted in his seat and maneuvered himself to pull up the fabric of his kilt so he could see where a chunk was missing. Damn. He had a big snout shaped, raggedy rip out of the cloth of his kilt. Plus, his truck was dead on the side of the road. Double damn.

Cassidy eased the car to the shoulder of the road, snatched up her phone, and dialed out. Her body was stiff and on point, her features grim. Finally someone answered the other end and she relaxed her shoulders enough to allow her body to rest back into the seat.

"Jon. Thank heavens you answered." She paused, listening. "Yes, well, there's a little glitch in our day. I'm guessing Ben's truck broke down on the side of the road between Murdock's and the office." She looked to Ben for confirmation.

Ben concurred.

"Somehow Ben instinctively went to Knight's for help." She glared at Ben then, letting him see her disapproval while Jon spoke on the other end. "Yeah, well the faster you find that truck and haul it to the office, the more likely Ben will have *any* truck *at all* by the end of the day."

Listening, she paused. "Thank you, Jon. Keep me posted, will you?"

She hit "end" on her phone and slipped it into the bag at her side. "Jon's got this. He'll have the truck returned to your place in a jiffy." She glanced sideways at him before continuing. "After that, we'll see what's what with the engine."

Ben consented. He was glad she knew what to do. She was something else. Smart, too.

"It's a good thing I came looking for you. What the heck were you thinking going to Charlie's for help?" Her forehead scrunched up in irritation. "Don't you know . . .?" The words hung out in the wind. She glanced back at him and visibly wilted. "No, I guess you don't remember." She looked back at the road in front of her. "Sorry. I lost my head there for a minute seeing you running like that."

Ben laughed, without a hint of humor. "Ah guess Ah donae run much either, aye?"

"You run. But it's more. . ." She tilted her head to the side in thought. "It's more controlled. More calculated. Scheduled."

Ben was not amused. "Please, explain that to me, lass. How on God's green earth can a stretch o' the legs in the mornin' sunshine be calculated?"

Cassidy laughed, shaking her head in wonder as a smile grew on her lips. "I don't know, Ben, I can't explain that to myself. You just do. You run maybe three or five days a week. Always at six in the morning, with the proper running gear. You carry two full bottles of water out and come back with two bottles emptied."

Her smile amazed him. "Wha' is proper gear faer running?"

Cassidy lifted a shoulder. "Eh. The usual. T-shirt, wicking of course. Running shorts or pants if it's cold out. Shoes, iPod, whistle."

"Wha' the hell do Ah need a whistle for?"

"You know, it's typical hiking gear. You do that, too. Hike. You lead hiking tours during the warmer seasons." Cassidy slammed down on the steering wheel. "Crappit! I wasn't supposed to tell you any of that!"

Outraged, Ben challenged her. "Why the hell not?"

"Doctor's orders." Cassidy's shoulders drooped. She glanced his way, a frown replacing her happier demeanor. "We're supposed to let you remember on your own, not define life for you. You know?" She reached past the steering wheel to signal her return to the road, glanced in the side mirror for approaching cars, and eased them back into motion. "It's meant to keep you from getting muddled up in the way we think things are or should be in your life."

Ben slouched in his seat as Cassidy turned the car to a street on the left. "I don' need a damn whistle. Ah've been whistlin' on mah own since I was a wee lad barely able t' walk."

Cassidy didn't miss a beat. "Sure you have." She slid a doubtful smile out of the corner of her mouth in his direction.

In turn, Ben puckered his lips and let out a sound that echoed off the interior walls of the car.

Cassidy slammed to a halt smack dab in the middle of the road.

"For the love of . . ." She covered her ears and rubbed. Her eyes were big and her forehead wrinkled in anger. "Please warn me before you *ever* do that again."

A car horn sounded directly behind them.

"Ah guess I donnae usually whistle, then?"

She shook her head, still rubbing her ears. "I can't say I've ever seen or heard you do that before."

Quiet permeated the car.

Ben waved to the car behind them to pass and offered a nod of apology as they drove by.

He looked out the side window and let his mind wander back to his earlier thoughts. "D'you wonder why it is, lass, that I can remember how t' drive mah truck but I donnae remember a thing about who Ah 'm or where Ah've come from?"

Cassidy ogled him incredulously, then sighed and relaxed against the back of her own seat. The car continued to idle, her foot on the brake. "Ben," she sighed. "There's no rhyme or reason to what you're remembering and what you're locking away inside your mind. You've been through some trauma. Just give it time. You'll be fine."

"Ah don' even know mah own name, Cassi." His face grew sad. "At least no' that Ah remember, anyway. I only know 'twas written on mah driver's license."

Cassidy smiled at him. She reached over to place her hand on top of his where it lay against his thigh. "You called me Cassi." She squeezed his hand. Tenderness played across her face. "You haven't called me that since second grade."

Ben liked this warmer side of Cassidy, especially the softness of her touch. He turned his hand over and clasped her fingers inside of his own, relishing the feel of them in his grasp. "Wha's second grade?"

Cassidy laughed out loud. "Fair enough," she said, smiling at him and letting him see her kindness as she leaned back into her own seat. "Second grade is a level of school that we attended together, you and I. We were roughly seven years old. It was the year you gave me a piece of red construction paper in the shape of a heart on Valentine's Day. You called me Cassi on the piece of paper."

When she smiled at him he could see it was a cherished and lovely memory, one she obviously held close to her heart.

Cassidy pulled her hand from his grasp and seemed to withdraw deep inside herself by looking away where he couldn't see her face.

"Did Ah say anythin' else to you? On the Valentine?"

She nodded.

"Will y' no' tell me wha' it said, then?"

Cassidy wiggled in her seat.

Ben perceived she was uncomfortable, so he adjusted his seatbelt and angled his body sideways in order to see her more clearly while he waited for her response.

Cassidy sniffled. She appeared more interested in watching for traffic as she focused her eyes beyond the car, but her actions gave her away as she attempted to wipe her face secretly. Once satisfied with her results, she offered Ben a sideways glance before rolling her eyes in defeat. With no traffic in sight, she put the car back into gear and proceeded forward. Finally, hiding behind her right hand like it was a blinder so he couldn't see her face, she gave him the answer he waited for. "It said in painstakingly beautiful print, 'I love you, my Cassi. Benjamin.'"

Ben comprehended by way of her behavior in the past twenty-four hours that clearly the sentiments of that second grade Valentine's note had never come true in their adult world. "Was tha' the only time Ah've expressed mah feelings t' you, love?"

Cassidy was quiet for several miles, appearing to be lost in an inner battle. Ben didn't press her. For the longest time he sat still, letting her stay away. In the silence, he decided he would make it a point to call her Cassi from then on. Perhaps that bit of tenderness would goad her into staying put when he reached out to touch her now and again. The idea satisfied him and he felt encouraged despite the distance between them at the moment.

Finally, when he was certain she wouldn't answer the question, he excused her. "'Twas a lang time ago."

Cassidy nodded while wiping at another tear threatening to fall. She sniffed and continued down a road he wasn't familiar with, though he could see the river straight ahead.

"Have you been to Skyline?"

"Skyline Mountain Road?"

Cassidy's eyes jumped with excitement. "You remember it then?"

Ben shook his head, sadly. "It's on mah license."

She wilted. They drove on in the quiet sounds of the road, the whir of wheel to pavement, and an occasional squeak of the front end responding to a dip in the road.

After a few minutes, Ben lost patience with the quiet. "Where were y' goin' when y' saw me on th' side o' the road?"

"I was running a quick errand into Huntsville. I didn't think you'd need me before I got back." Her cheeks glowed red in embarrassment. "I guess I was wrong to think that."

"D' you still need t' go there?"

She nodded, though without much energy. "I do. But Jon's meeting us at the office with your truck soon."

Ben mulled an idea around in his mind. "Can Ah go along for th' ride when you go, Cassi?"

She glanced a wary eye in his direction. "I guess so. Any reason why?"

"Ah believe I've got an errand of my own t' run." Ben smiled and nodded to himself, confirming his own thoughts before sitting back to enjoy the rest of the ride. He draped an arm along the base of the window and relaxed. Yes sir, he had an errand of his own to take care of. And today was the right day to do it.

***

Upon arriving in Huntsville, Ben had the forethought to ask Cassidy to drop him off at an intersection near where he needed to go, but far enough as to not give himself away. From there he hiked to the Dodge dealership and proceeded to deal with a salesman for a brand spanking new truck. He'd seen enough evidence on Cassidy's desk that morning to know he had some money. His driver's license assured him he owned some land. And by golly by all that was holy, he needed a new truck. One thing he remembered for certain was that the Dodge Ram was outfitted with a Hemi. And he wanted a

Hemi. He could feel it in his soul, God bless him!

But by the time the salesman verified his accounts and handed him the keys, Cassidy was front and center, tapping her toes, arms crossed. The bank had somehow notified her of his purchase and she'd known exactly where to find him.

Ben simply raised an eyebrow back at her and commanded, "You can follow me back t' th' river, Cassi, my love."

The smile he gave her didn't make a dent in her armor, but that little *my love* part he added on made her visibly go soft as a petal. He gave her a wink and they were off, heading back for home, one behind the other.

Once in Riverland, having been allowed time to think, Ben decided the one place he needed to check out more than any other was that address on his driver's license. Maybe it held clues to help him regain his memory. He pulled up to the curb in front of the office and jumped down from his truck to greet Cassidy. She was busy angling her own car next to where Jon, true to his word, had left Ben's dead truck.

Ben, quick to act, was already opening Cassidy's door when she turned off the ignition. "Let's go up t' th' mountain and see wha' we can find, shall we?" He wiggled his eyebrows at her, entreating her to agree.

Cassidy pulled herself out of the car along with the package she'd picked up in the city. She looked up at the sky. "We don't have much daylight left, Ben. Are you sure you don't want to wait and go early tomorrow so you have time to explore the property?"

He scanned the late afternoon sky. A bank of clouds loomed on the horizon. "How long does it take to drive there?"

"Oh, not long. Twenty minutes or so? But you won't have a lot of time to scout it out. Maybe a half hour, if that."

"A half hour is long enough to ge' mah first glimpse o' it." He paused in thought before nodding his certainty that they did in fact have enough time. "Ah'm jus' curious t' see it. Maybe it holds a clue or two for my mem'ry banks."

"Well then, let me put these things in the office and we'll get going."

Cassidy did as planned, but when she met him at the truck, a funny thing happened. Ben opened the door for her to climb in and, well, she was short. Too short. So she busied herself by placing a knee on the floorboard of the truck and was preparing to lift herself up into the cab by holding onto the seatbelt when Ben saw his opportunity.

"Oh no you don', lass. Ah canno' ha' you fallin' out o' my truck before you've ev'n got inside it." He pushed an arm under her knees and pulled her back to fall into his chest.

Cassidy squealed. "You can't pick me up Ben! Your head!"

"Aye lass, but Ah can and Ah did." He wiggled his eyebrows playfully. "Pu' your arm aroun' mah neck, love. Ah'll lift you into your seat."

When Cassidy followed his instructions, Ben felt the need to protect her, to reel her in, to claim her. He wanted to keep her close, tight, for himself.

"We won't be able to see your land well if you don't put me in that truck and get us driving down the road, Ben." She dropped her head to the side, questioning him.

"Right, A'm driving us t' th' mountain." Lordy, but she was a beautiful creature, even more so in his arms.

"Only if you put me in the truck and get yourself buckled in, too."

He let his eyes fall to her mouth. Need roared to life inside him. He considered briefly what would happen if he carried her off to his room. Her tongue eased out and licked her top lip. His body responded in turn, involuntarily pushing a low growl from deep inside his chest. Her tongue captivated him. She ran it across the pink planes of her lower lip before pulling it back inside. "You're drivin' me ou' o' my min' with your mouth, Cassi."

Her eyes grew big in response as she watched what he would do. Finally, she pushed against his shoulders emphatically. "Get with the program, Ben. You bought this truck. Let's see what it can do!"

CHAPTER FIVE

Ben drove, with the help of Cassidy's directions, up the mountain to his Skyline Mountain Road property. Clouds bumped into the higher elevated landscape and brought a colder bite to the air. The drab colors of the sky washed everything in gloom and sadness. The water that leaked from the rocks lining the mountain road looked thicker here, indicating a potential freeze in the near future.

Cassidy sat on the far side of the cab, lost in managerial tasks, texting and amending a reservation with guests due to arrive later that month. For Ben, the trek up the curving, winding roads gave him time and opportunity to think.

As the miles passed by, the distance between homes grew. Some were old and well maintained, others seemed to beg the earth to swallow them whole, to put an end to their misery. Ben wondered, what was his own house like? Old, new, or somewhere in between? Fresh and clean, refurbished, what? But only one question remained upon their arrival. Why was Skyline Mountain Road listed as his place of residence on his driver's license when all that remained was a mailbox and a panoramic view of sky, land, and valley below?

Trees creaked and moaned their discontent with the cold as Ben and Cassidy exited the truck. Cassidy didn't waste any time and took off for the edge of the property. Ben was grateful for the distance she gave him to take it all in.

He breathed in deeply and let his eyes scan the area. Bugger, but this was an empty place. It looked like a nice enough piece of land, though abandoned to the elements. But for what reason? A section of earth was scratched out where a house once stood. In the center of the area facing the road was a dip in the dirt, obviously worn from use. Probably where the front steps were previously located if the crepe myrtle tree, gnarled with vines, was any witness. Neglect is what that poor tree signified and it stabbed at his heart.

When Ben approached the place where the back of the house once stood, he noticed Cassidy angling herself over the low-lying stone wall that lined the rear of the property. When positioned on the other side, she eased down onto the hard surface and sat, looking out over the landscape beyond. Ben turned around to scan the width of the property. It was a good piece of land, but it needed tending. Barren kudzu vines coiled willy-nilly, a true sign of trouble. But if it was cleaned up, it could be something. Maybe it could be the place for a new house. A new home. A new family.

Ben looked back to where Cassidy sat studying the valley below. He ambled over and took a seat straddling the wall near her. Cassidy shuddered in the cold. Ben followed her eyes and marveled at the million-dollar view.

"It's a fine place for a home."

Cassidy turned to him, smiled sadly. "It's the best view Skyline has to offer."

"Why's that?"

"You can see the peak of Skyline better than anyone around." Cassidy aimed her head in the direction of where someone was working on the Skyline Christmas sign. She pulled a hand out of her pocket to point down past the naked trees that filled the mountainside. "You can see all of Riverland as easily, too. It's the best of both worlds." She pushed her hand back into her pocket and visibly shivered.

Ben nodded and focused his attention back at the space between him and the road. "There was a house at one time."

"Yes, there was a house."

He looked at her then, eye to eye. "Tell me what you know of the house, Cassi. Was it a house full of happiness?"

"I don't know. It was empty after your grandfather died. You had it bulldozed two years ago."

"Why's that?"

"Your truck couldn't make it up here in bad weather so you couldn't live here. And besides, it was kind of falling apart at the seams. Dangerous even. Too many broken windows and sagging boards. The roof was starting to fall in. Someone was bound to get hurt, you said."

Sadness threaded through her words. Ben saw the full picture she painted and made a sound of acknowledgment.

"You don't recall any of it?"

Ben aimed his head in the direction of where the house would've been. Hope jumped in his chest reaching for something to jump-start his memory. "No' e'en a bit."

Cassidy sighed and stood to walk away. "I'm cold. I need to move and warm up." The wind gusted and made her lose her balance. Ben caught her, catching her off guard, and pulled her into his lap, wrapping her in his arms as he did so.

"Sorry." Embarrassment colored her face with red.

Ben grinned wickedly. "Sorry is th' last thing Ah'm, lass."

He moved her hair away from her eyes. The wind wreaked havoc on it, whipping it around her head here and there. Cassidy pushed her face into his hand at the first touch of his warmth.

"Oh, you are so warm. Both hands please."

Ben extended his other hand and enveloped her face in his heat.

She sighed her contentment.

As Ben held her face and watched her nestling into his grasp, he was drawn into her softness again, her gentleness, her lack of gall. She was so fair and lovely. Her eyes fluttered open. She smiled up at him as he closed the distance between them. She sucked in a breath of surprise as he touched her lips with his own, testing, then teasing. Cassidy didn't return his explorations right away, but she didn't run. He leaned back to study her eyes. Something in them showed her fear but she held still in his hands.

He ran a thumb across her bottom lip. "Ah want t' know you, Cassi. Ah want t' remember who y'are t' me, love. Ah'd like t' think we're good toge'er, you and Ah."

Cassidy began shaking her head but he stilled her.

"Wha'ever was before, le' us forget jus' now." Ben touched her then, again easing himself across her lips. And when he heard her sigh and felt her lean slightly forward, he pulled her closer and took to her mouth like a starving man.

Cassidy's hands slipped up his chest and beyond, wrapping around his neck. Ben eased his hands down to her hips to pull her tight, letting her feel his response. His tongue danced around hers. He breathed in her scent and took the fleshy softness of her backside into his hands and squeezed. Cassidy moaned. Ben continued laving her mouth and allowed his body to direct them. He stood and lifted his leg over the wall, backed them up together against the hard cold surface, and as he eased down to sit again, he pushed her legs to either side, wrapping her body to straddle his own.

Cassidy tried to complain, but he shushed her with further kisses across her cheeks as he traveled around to nip at her neck, whispering senseless words along the way. Words of pleasure and praise, entreaties of openings and takings. Holding her steady with one hand, he let the other roam to weigh her breast. He squeezed gently, looking back into her eyes, watching for approval. She appeared lost in pleasure as he slipped a thumb across her hard nipple, provoking it to reach for his mouth. "Aye, tha' you were wearin' skirts, Ah'd be in y' already, givin' you mah full hilt, lass."

Cassidy gasped then. Ben took her nipple into his mouth through her clothes and tugged, gently scraping his teeth across it as he receded back. Cassidy's hand gripped his shoulders and then she gave him a push.

"You want me to stop, lass?"

Dazed and confused, Cassidy came back to the present quickly. She leapt off his lap. "Oh God. No! Sorry. I mean yes! Yes. Stop." She frantically brushed her hands at her flyaway hair, busied herself with zipping her jacket, closing herself off from him.

"Aye, now lassie. There's no need t' be like tha'."

"Like what?"

Not for the first time Ben watched her face flush before she reeled in her emotions, spun to leap over the wall, and marched towards the truck with her back up straight.

Ben sighed. *There she goes again. Running away from me.* He looked over his shoulder to see her hips swaying to the beat of his blood, making him laugh out loud. "Aye, now tha's th' way of i'. You tease me ye' again."

REMEMBERING SKYLINE

After walking around the mountaintop, measuring and imagining, Ben settled Cassidy in the passenger side of the truck before entering on the driver's side. The heat was warm pushing past the vents into their faces. He sat looking out across the valley one last time, lost in thought. Cassidy waited at his side patiently, warming her hands in the heat the truck offered, her feet dangling from the seat, too short for reaching the floorboards.

"I remember my Mam-maw used to stand at a window overlooking that view there." He nodded to himself, absorbed by the memory. "She would wash dishes and sing hymns through the open window to anything beyond its panes that would listen. Paw-paw would stand in the hallway door and watch her without letting on he was nearby. When she would finish the song she'd tell him thank you for listening. He'd applaud her before taking her into his arms for a spin around the kitchen floor. She would laugh." He paused. Sadness sat on his shoulders. "God, I'll never forget the sound of her laughter. She was so beautiful the way she laughed at his carryings on." Ben turned and looked at Cassidy watching him. "Mah gran'parents were amazing people, weren't they, lass." It wasn't a question, but rather a statement of fact.

Cassidy nodded in agreement, letting him remember the good times. "Yes. They were amazing."

Ben slipped the truck into gear. "Tha's all Ah remember."

"No. I don't think so." Cassidy looked strange. Confounded, even.

"No? Wha' d' you mean, love?"

"You remembered to speak in plain English. No brogue."

"Aye. Ah suppose Ah did do that."

They headed back down the side of the mountain together, hope invading past the mountainside all the way into the cab of the truck.

***

When morning broke for Cassidy the next day (around the time a rooster rolls over and pulls his blanket back up over his head) she hit the finance books and stock exchange reports, desperate to find a way to cover for the expense of a brand new Dodge Ram 3500 Hemi. She didn't much care that it could lift the Titanic out of the river or haul a trailer house to some park nearby. She didn't even care that it could make it up the mountain in the aftermath of an ice storm. She wouldn't be around to see any of that if Ben came back into his right mind and found that she had let him spend umpteen-bazillion-dollars on a truck he never would've bought in his wildest dreams. No siree, she wasn't going to live to tell her grandkids because he would kill her on the spot if he ever found out she was the one who had Power of Attorney when he bought that ginormous truck currently sitting in the driveway. Right next to the one he loved. The one that cost him pennies to repair on any given day. Without the help of Charlie Knight. The one his grandfather had given him along with his first driver's license way too many years ago.

By eight that morning she was on coffee pot number two with a solution in sight when Ben walked into the office and stretched all his kilted wares out in front of her to see. God but he was a handsome devil, which was why she ignored him completely.

Ben pouted.

The landline rang and after answering, Cassidy handed the phone to Ben, still focused on the numbers of her plan. "It's for you."

Ben took the phone from her. "G'morning."

Someone on the other end spoke.

Ben looked puzzled. "Th' return is two days late, y' say?"

Again a pause for someone to respond. In detail, apparently.

Concern began to spike Ben's words. "Th' jackets, vests, and accessories were returned t' your store wi'out the kilts three days ago?"

Cassidy looked up from her computer screen, on full alert.

Ben placed a hand over the phone, hiding his words from the caller. Tension bunched his forehead. "Di' y' know the kilts were rentals, love?"

"Oh. That." Cassidy pushed her chair back and then stood to walk around the desk. She took the phone from him and shooed him off toward the coffee pot. "Go! I've got this."

She gave him another nod of the head to encourage him. Ben walked away questioning her, so she turned her back to him, lowering her voice so he couldn't hear her end of the conversation.

"Hello. This is Cassidy Spencer, Mr. Murray's business manager. I'm really very sorry, but I'm going to have to apologize. There's been a little bit of a hiccup." She paused, then laughed nervously. She angled her head to eye Ben and verify that he couldn't hear her.

Ben was manning a hot cup of coffee and his attention was fixed on something beyond her view outside the window.

"Mr. Murray suffered a little bit of an accident that caused him to lose his memory. And well, umm, he kind of sort of thought he owned those kilts?"

Silence.

Cassidy's head bobbed up and down, affirming whatever was said on the other end of the line. "Yes ma'am, that's exactly right. He has forgotten everything. Well, mostly everything." Hopefully, the rental agent understood the dilemma entirely. "And I didn't realize someone else had already returned part of the order to you." Cassidy laughed nervously before continuing. "Sorry, it's been a little crazy, what with his memory and all."

Ben walked past her towards the supply room and quietly mouthed "Aunt Patty returned a few things the day after New Year's before I could stop her."

"If he has *forgotten,* then I'm sure two hundred and five dollars A DAY rental fee for EACH suit will help him remember *just fine!"*

Ben directed a raised eye at Cassidy as the yelling came through the wires loud and clear.

Cassidy held the phone away from her ear, jerking as the last few words shrilled loudly. She cautiously replaced the receiver back to her ear to respond. "I will handle this right away."

The voice on the other end continued in loud form. "I have another wedding party waiting in line for those kilts so until the entire order is returned, the *entire* price is in effect for *each and every day!*"

"Yes sir. I mean, ma'am. I understand." Cassidy remembered the kilt Ben was wearing when he had been attacked by Charlie's dog. "Out of curiosity, how much would it be to purchase one of the kilts?"

The response that came through the lines may as well have presented the woman in person for all the presence it brought into the room with its voluminous shout. *"Those kilts are NOT for sale!"*

"Yes ma'am! I understand clearly." Cassidy stood at attention, holding back a ridiculous need to salute. "I'll have them back to you within the hour, sir. I mean ma'am. Sir." She jerked as an exploding sound rang from the earpiece announcing a disconnect on the other end.

"Well." She eyed the phone before gently replacing it to its rest.

Ben stood undaunted, watching for her response.

Cassidy mirrored his demeanor, quietly trying to construct an explanation. She busied her hands with tracing the outline of the phone's earpiece as she thought.

"So my cousin's wedding went off without a hitch, then?"

Cassidy jerked her head up to look him in the eye.

"It's all right, Cass. I remember standing up for them on New Year's Day, ringing in the year with two hundred other witnesses."

"You do?"

"Yes," he nodded. "Did the bride's family make it back t' Scotland okay?"

Cassidy agreed quietly. Clearly his brogue was slipping away.

Ben walked back to the window and sighed. "I seem t' remember you weren't there, Cass. Why's that?"

Cassidy's stomach hurt. He'd fallen back into calling her Cass like all the other locals. Her heart squeezed inside her chest. She circled the desk and sat down behind it, placing her head in her hands, hiding from him in case he turned back around. "I'm sorry, Ben. I just couldn't."

"You weren't secretly pining for my cousin or anything, were you?"

"No. I'm not *pining away* over your cousin." She wanted to bang her head on the wood surface but she couldn't do that anymore than she could look into Ben's mossy eyes and tell him she was *pining* away for him. *Lordy but would this torturous love in her heart ever end?*

Ben threw back the last of his coffee. "Well, I guess that solves the mystery of the bridal company on caller ID!"

Cassidy swung her head up in response. "Wait. You've been checking our calls?"

Ben grunted. "It's business, Cass. You checked for numbers, too, right?"

"Well, yes, but. . ."

Ben reached over to ruffle her hair like he'd done a million times throughout her life. "It's okay. It's what we do around here to check for missed reservation calls, right?" He chuckled then winked at her before turning to leave. "I'm going to go drive my new truck and fit it out with my supplies and such." He stopped short of the door and turned back to face her. "You wouldn't happen to know what happened to my cell phone, would you?"

Cassidy recovered it from the desk drawer and laid it on top for him to examine. "It's dead though. I don't know where your charger is."

Ben stepped back to the desk and pocketed his phone. "Now *that*, I do know. It's in my old truck. I just didn't know what it went to until now." And with that he waved off as if nothing was out of the ordinary in their world.

Cassidy looked back at the computer monitor and determined it was time to make some money, and *fast. Risks be damned!*

CHAPTER SIX

Ben pried Cassidy out of the office approximately an hour after the sun went down, promising her a surprise made in heaven, a picnic on the mountain underneath the stars. In the warmth of his truck, of course. The clouds had moved past late in the afternoon but they left a bone-piercing cold in their wake. But he'd come through for her honestly, she thought, as she bit into the best bite of barbeque the south had to offer. Straight from Henry's kitchen. Ben supplied her with a side of beans and potato salad, too, and a pickle sitting on top of her pulled pork exactly how she liked it. That he'd remembered the pickle made her feel all warm and fuzzy inside. Things were looking up.

On that note, she internally patted herself on the back for the quick investment turnaround she'd made earlier in the day. At ten that morning she'd bought, by three in the afternoon she'd sold, and doubled half of Ben's liquid assets, more than making up for his shopping spree. Not bad for a day full of number playing. Not bad at all. Best of all, he'd never miss a dime for spending it on that fancy new truck they were sitting in, either, since she'd also paid off the loan he'd taken out.

"It's a little warm in here for my comfort level. Would you like to join me under the stars in the bed of the truck?" He wiggled his eyebrows at her suggestively. "I've got plenty of blankets to keep you warm."

Cassidy laughed at him. "Is that what you meant when you said you left to stock your truck this morning?" She goosed him in his side, riling and teasing him. "You're such a man!"

"I don't know what you're talking about!" Ben feigned ignorance, grinning wickedly. "I'm merely offering a front row seat showcasing the heavenly expanse."

"Pshaw! You've never been a good liar, Ben Murray! There's no sense starting that business now." She grinned, shaking her head at him in fun.

They climbed down out of the cab of the truck. Ben helped her into the back where he revealed a masterfully planned layout of blankets, pillows, and comfort for stargazing. Once she was comfortable against the pillow-lined cab of the truck, Ben settled in next to her and pulled her close. They sat in silence for the longest time, watching, waiting for the heavens to move. The stars were in full regalia for the evening, the cold atmosphere showcasing them in their diamond bright brilliance.

Cassidy didn't know what to do with herself. Sure, she'd been this close to Ben before, especially so in the past few days, though usually it was more of a brother–sister occasion.

But their world was new and unproven now, unknown. It was shaky and risky and uncertain, unlike the numbers she'd spent her day with. Numbers were reliable. Love was not. This situation didn't make her feel altogether safe. She knew firsthand that tomorrow could bring an entirely new set of circumstances, likely the very same problems she tried to run away from only three days ago. She wasn't kidding herself. She did love Ben. Yes, she loved him with all her heart. In fact, she couldn't remember what it was like *not* to love Ben Murray. He may not have intentionally returned her love, except for that one little Valentine's Day paper heart with the handwriting of a young boy, but he was always up in the big middle of her life for every joy, celebration, and even the unfortunate events of life. He was there for her whether he wanted to admit it or not. But she wanted more. No, that wasn't true. She *needed* more. She *needed* to be loved and adored openly and for all to see. She *needed* to be praised and relished in every way by her man.

Cassidy redirected her attention back to Ben who was intent on watching the sky, certain he'd spot a meteor in the cold Alabama night. His mind was void of any memory of her shortcomings or long suits and he'd somehow lost years of data on her. But something existed, safely tucked away inside his mind, something enough to drive him to pull her close in this little disturbance of his life. She was glad to be there with him.

Cassidy snuggled in closer to Ben's side and shivered.

"Are you warm enough?" He looked down into her eyes as he eased the blanket tighter around her shoulders. His gaze dipped to watch as she ran her tongue across her lips.

"I'm okay so long as you keep me close." She smiled.

Ben reached and smoothed a hand across her face, holding her cheek in its warmth. "I'll keep you warm, Cassi." He bent his face to hers, paused, and touched her lips with his own softly. He leaned back enough for words to escape him, and whispered to her and the whole universe, "I promise."

With those two words, Cassidy lost all inhibition and pushed herself forward to take anything and everything Ben Murray could give her this cold winter's night. Because it could be that *this* night was the only time she would ever have her man. Without Ben, her life was empty and colder than anything the world could offer her. Should tomorrow come and Ben walk away from her for the remembering, then she would at least have tonight. She would have given her all. She would move forward either way.

***

Ben collapsed on top of Cassi, breathing heavily, trying desperately to make his chest calm down to a reasonable rhythm. He couldn't remember ever being so entirely satiated than he was in this moment with Cassi under the stars. He rolled away from her without letting go such that she stayed wrapped together with him. Ben draped an arm over his head and counted his breathing to help it steady. When he could finally find his voice, he asked, "Are you okay?"

Cassidy didn't say a word, she merely nudged his shoulder and let her arm rest across his chest in a heap of exhaustion.

"I didn't hurt you, did I?" Ben squeezed her, forcing her to look into his face for him to see for himself. He scanned her eyes, her mouth. "Never in my life would I want to hurt you, Cassi."

A single tear ran down Cassidy's face, catching the light of the stars above.

Ben caught the droplet on his fingertip, puzzled and a little bit alarmed. "Why are you crying?"

Again, she didn't say anything but rather lifted her shoulder in uncertainty. Their eyes caught and both understood instinctively what the other felt. There were simply too many unknowns. Too much uncertainty.

Ben pulled her head back to lay on his shoulder and sighed. They peered into the night empty of the world and hoping for the heavens to declare their mission, their purpose. High above them, in the expanse of the sky, a light shot across the entire blanket of night for them both to witness.

Ben squeezed Cassidy tight. "See. There's something spectacular waiting for us up ahead." He looked at her again. "Something special for you and me. Together, Cassidy. I think we were meant to be in this place together." He pointed upwards. "The sky agrees." He smiled, looking back at her, then nodded as if saying, *it is so*.

Cassidy hadn't agreed with him, but she hadn't disagreed, either. Ben let that settle over him and laid still for what seemed an eternity, imagining what it could be like to have Cassidy wrapped up in his life forever. When he heard her breathing settle in for the night, he simply followed her to dreamland on top of his mountain. He let his mind take charge casting his future for a little while. The sun would come up tomorrow soon enough. Then he'd make some real decisions.

CHAPTER SEVEN

Ben pulled up to the edge of the wall at his property on Skyline Mountain Road mid-morning. He'd settled Cassidy back in at the office earlier, before the light of day had opportunity to appear. She'd been quiet, but seemed pleasant after the night's events. Ben aimed his new truck in the direction of the sky at the stone wall's edge. Bolton Matthews, a childhood friend who'd been too busy in his own life to stay in touch, pulled right alongside of him, and then jumped out to greet him like old friends.

"Man! I never would've thought this day would happen." Bolton slapped a hand into Ben's, shaking it vigorously.

Ben, a bit confused, shook back. "Why's that?"

Bolton slipped his hand into his pocket for warmth and resumed an easy stance. "Well, you know. It's been a long time, is all."

Ben let it go at face value and concentrated on his reason for calling Bolton to the mountaintop. "So, I'm wondering what it would cost me to build a new home on this spot.

Something like my grandparents' old home, but updated with modern conveniences. Do you think you can spec it out and give me an estimate?"

"Sure, I can." Bolton smiled with relief lacing the edges of his face. "It *is* my business after all." He chuckled. "Tell me what you want and I'll calculate what I can do pricewise. How does that sound?"

The two of them put their heads together over the blueprints Ben provided of his grandparents' old home. They spent the following hour walking the position of the structure on the land itself. They took some measurements, threw out ideas between them, mulling over possibilities but maintaining the concept of the original home. About the time they were sitting on the tailgate of the truck, talking textiles and finishes, Jon and Cassidy arrived in her car, both looking pretty worried. Bear pulled in right behind them in his old beater truck, dressed for business.

"Hey guys! What's up?" Ben hopped off the gate and hustled to greet them. Bolton held back, waiting for the dust to settle with the new arrivals.

Jon slapped Ben's shoulder in a brotherly not-so-close-but-close-enough-hug, all the while aiming a watchful eye in Bolton's direction. "Bolton." He spoke low and motioned his head in recognition of the other man's attendance.

Bear, not so eloquent, stood with feet rooted to the ground, knees slightly bent, hands lightly splayed on hips ready for a fight. "What the hell's going on here?"

Cassidy looked like she wanted to be anywhere but on that particular mountain.

Ben aimed his attention at Cassidy. "Is everything okay, Cassi?"

Both Jon and Bear let no time pass before pushing past Ben, proceeding straight to Bolton, hackles up, ready to take him down.

"What the hell, guys?" Ben followed, confusion quickly turning to anger.

Jon pushed Bolton's shoulder. "What are you up to, Bolton?" He waited ten seconds, then blazed forward. Jon's jaw twitched like it always did right before he lost all control. "Did you think because you found me a deal on some reclaimed floors you could win our good graces? Huh? You think you've paid for your sins now? Or are you trying to take advantage of Ben while he's down, huh?"

Ben pushed between the two men, forcing some space between them. "What do you mean take advantage of me? I asked Bolton to meet me here to talk business, man! Back off!"

Bear stood three feet away, his emotions barely in check, ready to pounce if given half a chance.

Ben gave Bear the evil eye. "You too, man." He held Bear's attention without flinching. "Cassidy. Explain."

Cassidy stepped up to his side and pleaded with him. "Ben, we were alarmed. We don't want you doing anything you might regret later, is all."

"Regret? You think I would regret building a modern version of my grandparents' home here on this mountain?" Ben was completely confused by what was happening. "Why would I regret that, Cassidy?"

Before Cassidy could respond, Bear leapt. "I'll tell you why you'd regret it. This lowlife doesn't deserve to spit on your shoes much less rebuild your home after what he's done."

"What has he done?" Ben's voice was beginning to rise with frustration.

Bear gave Bolton a direct shove towards the wall, backing it up with his whole body shoving harder.

Jon was right there with him. Side by side, Bear and Jon were forcing Bolton backwards, dangerously close to the edge of the drop-off.

"Let them deal with this, Ben." Cassidy tugged at Ben's sleeve. She pleaded with him with her eyes. "They know what they're doing. Bolton, too. Come with me and let them be."

Ben's irritation skyrocketed. He was sick and tired of his friends trying to "handle" him. He wasn't stupid. He knew they'd been withholding information from him so he had time to regain his own memories. But picking a fight with a man that had done nothing to hurt anyone else was wrong. He set Cassidy aside, told her to let him handle his own fight, and then off he went to push his friends each into their own corners so they could all work out this misunderstanding like grown-ass adults. But when he stepped into the mix, fists flew. He pushed himself into the fray as Jon's fist aimed for Bolton's face, and, slamming into Ben instead, pummeled him toward the ground. The wall between it and him jutted out a fraction, enough to catch his head before he could find the earth. Ben's head hit the stone. He wilted from there, hitting the cold hard dirt with a thud.

A loud gasp invaded the air as Cassidy watched the whole testosterone-laden episode play out in front of her. All three men left standing stood watching in horror as Ben splayed across the cold dirt of the mountain. Time hung between them all, counting off the hour-long seconds once again, giving them each time to sort out their own reactions.

Cassidy landed on Ben first, checking for a pulse, for blood, for some semblance of life. Tears ran in rivers down her cheeks. Her nose dripped and she wiped unconsciously at it with the sleeve of her jacket. Her hands trembled as she ran them over the new injuries of his head.

Bear and Bolton were shouting overhead about girlfriends, babies, and some crazy nonsense. Jon crouched down next to Ben's side, waiting for Cassidy's orders.

Ben groaned. *Holy son of a . . . good gracious molly! Damn but my head hurts.* He reached up to touch his head, pulled back to inspect his fingers. No blood. Cassidy insistently prodded him, wanting to know how many fingers she was holding up. Jon bellowed out orders saying someone needed to call 911. Ben could barely make out a pair of work boots shuffling on the side with some brown oxfords, dirt flying all around the scuffle with words meant only for a late-night bar crowd to hear. He lifted himself up on his hands and knees and dragged in a deep breath. Maybe if he could breathe in and out he could stand up. He tried. He wavered back down. Jon caught him.

"Catch your breath, man. Sit still and catch your breath." Jon held Ben in place so he couldn't do anything but breathe, take in the details. He rolled his head to find Cassidy on his other side. Her tear-covered face said it all. She was scared to death. *But why?*

That's when the pieces all came together inside his brain like they were made of magnets clinging to each other to make sense of his life. Dicker's Christmas lights. The ladder. The emergency room at the hospital. Charlie Knight and his dog. His new truck. The star-lit night. Cassidy open to him, bare as the day she was born, and offering her body to him for pleasure and safekeeping. The wedding rings he'd taken out of the drawer this morning for the purpose of asking Cassidy to be his wife. They were his grandparents' wedding rings left to him for claiming his own love. Which was why he'd come up here together with Bolton on a whim and imagineered a modified family home for Cassidy from the prints left behind of the original Murray home on this very mountain plot. Bolton, the rat-snake who'd run off with another girl at the end of high school and left Bear's sister, Angel, heartbroken after an entire lifetime of planning to marry her and spend the rest of their lives together. A wash of nausea ran through his body and Ben felt like he was going to throw up. He closed his eyes and willed himself to pull it together.

Cassidy spoke softly to him. She smoothed her hand over his sleeve, reminding him she was on his side. "Ben, what can I do for you? What can we all do to help you?"

Ben sat back on his haunches, still taking in controlled breaths. He pinched the bridge of his nose, then followed up by wiping his cold, wind-chapped face with his hand, essentially pushing all of the day's complications away. Then he stood, with Jon's assistance, balanced himself, and braced his hands on his hips.

Bolton and Bear were twenty yards away still thrashing in the dirt, scraping out the past from each other's hides.

Jon watched Ben, ready to jump to his aid at the slightest indication of distress. Cassidy cried the worst kind of tears, silent tears. Painful tears. The kind of tears that ripped your soul apart while you're holding someone else together.

Ben turned and stretched one foot towards the road, set it in place and followed with the other foot, careful to stabilize himself before standing still. He took a deep breath, encouraged by his success so far. "I like the truck, by the way." He looked at Cassidy. "You like it, too, right?"

She nodded carefully.

Ben smiled at her, trying his damnedest to tell her everything would be all right.

She hesitantly smiled back.

"It'll maneuver this mountain easily enough, all the way through the winter months."

Ben opened his arms wide for his *Cassi*, and without delay, she stepped in, right where he wanted her to be. He rested his head on hers and spoke in a thick brogue tongue. "Cassi, for th' love o' all things holy, please won' y' make all mah dreams come true?"

Cassidy jerked back in shock to look into his face. "That's what you said to me that first night in the storeroom!"

"Aye, lass, I did."

She searched his eyes for mockery. "Are you sure you meant it?"

"When, love? Then or now?"

"Both." Her forehead wrinkled in worry. Her eyes dropped down and she fiddled with a button on his shirt. "You can't say something like that to me, Ben Murray."

"Why not, Cassi?" His smile reached out to her through the words, an attempt to pull her eyes back to his.

"Because." Cassidy looked away towards Ben's truck, a reminder of what they had been together, no doubt.

Ben followed her gaze. "Last night I loved you with all I had to give. And today I love you more, Cassi." Ben dropped down on one knee, failed, and ended up on two knees with both Jon and Cassidy trying to catch him. He brushed them off. "It's good. I'm good." He took Cassidy's hand into his and looked back up at her from bended knee. "This morning I took out a velvet box my grandfather gave to me and decided I would do something with it today."

She appeared to consider his words, watching him as she spoke. "I'm not sure I understand where you're going with this, Ben."

He drew in a long, deep breath of air, looked to Jon, and exhaled. Bear and Bolton were laying on the ground, moaning. He turned back to face her. "I mean to ask you to be my wife, Cassidy Spencer."

Cassidy gasped as she brought one hand to her throat. "You what?" New tears began to form and fall.

Ben nodded. "I love you more now than I ever could've in second grade. I've been too much a fool to say so. If you'll have my stubborn arse, I'd like for you to be my wife, to have my babies, and grow old together with me on this enduring mountain."

Jon pumped a fist into the air and shouted with joy, then started texting at the speed of light so all their family and friends were clued in.

Bolton and Bear groaned in harmony, "It's about damn time." They looked at each other, there in the dirt, and agreed. "Idiot!"

Cassidy's hands covered her mouth. Her head moved from side to side, slowly in disbelief.

Ben smiled, hopeful. "Does this mean yes, you will? No, you can't believe I'm finally coming to my senses?" Concern leaked into his eyes before continuing on. "Or is it a no, you won't take my hand in marriage? Please put me out of my misery, lass. Give me an answer to my question?"

Cassidy threw her arms around his shoulders and kissed the top of his head. "Yes, you big Scottish brogey! Yes! I would love to be your wife!"

Ben gingerly stood and then embraced the love of his life. "I will love you forever, Cassidy soon-to-be-Murray. Always and forever, I am yours." His eyes gleamed down at her. "I promise."

He set his lips to hers, sealed his love that very moment, letting her know he remembered all of her from the night before underneath the star-filled expanse. When Bear finally ambled himself over to join in the congratulations, Ben pulled back and commanded the men. "All this business about Bolton is over. *Finito.* Angel's a big girl, she can fend for herself."

Bear reluctantly agreed after a moment of consideration.

"Besides, I hear he's got his due." Jon piped up with a grin.

"What's that?" Bear asked.

Bolton painfully staggered into the mix. "I've got myself two kids and no wife. She left after running up all of my credit cards and emptying my bank accounts. I can barely order supplies for construction jobs."

"No kidding." Bear crossed his arms and glared at the man in question. "Karma and all that. Rough woman, that one."

"Speaking of money," Ben aimed at Cassidy.

As quick as possible, Cassidy escaped Ben and took off at a full run. "You can't pin me with anything!" she yelled over her shoulder.

When she'd put the truck between them, she added, "Besides, I doubled your assets yesterday! You're in better shape than ever and now you have a new truck that actually runs, too!"

The men all joined in and agreed with her.

Ben smiled and wondered at his good fortune.

"What's that stupid smile on your face for, Scotty?" Bear asked.

Ben angled his head in thought before answering. "Why did it take me so long to do anything about Cassidy, anyway?"

Jon answered without delay. "Your grandfather put the idea in your head that women weren't worth their trouble when your grandmother died."

"Why ever not?"

"Because she died on him, I guess?"

Ben shook his head in disbelief. "But she was seventy-four years old when she died."

"That's the pisser, man! They had a good long life together!"

"I don't understand." Ben was clearly out of the loop of what his grandfather's complaining centered around.

"She left him, Ben. It made him mad that she died. So in his grief he said they weren't worth the trouble."

"That's the dumbest thing I've ever heard!"

The three men rolled their eyes at Ben.

"I know, right?" Jon slapped him on the back. "It's about time you got it, my man."

"Why didn't somebody tell me?"

Everyone, Cassidy included, started stepping all over their words explaining in great detail how stubborn he really was.

***

Five weeks later, the soonest Ben could rent a kilt and run down some Scottish thistle and heather, Benjamin Thomas Murray carried his woman, his one and only Valentine, Cassidy Murray over the threshold at The River Rat Boat Rentals and Cottages, Cottage No. 7, the honeymoon suite.

Everyone they loved was in attendance at their wedding. Mama Paula gushed over Ben behind the scenes, making sure he had the right jacket and accessories, plus an appropriate gift for Cassidy. She'd even given him a mother–son talk in the absence of his own mother. Bear grumbled about it, but he booked a flight back from Italy for the big event. He'd said that seeing his own woman, Julia, made up for the hardship. Jon, Christy, and Rudi, along with Bolton and his two children celebrated the day together with them, too. Even Dicker made an appearance in the far corners of the chapel. Four of Bear's sisters surrounded Angel on the third row of the groom's side. Mama Paula's pride shone for all the world to see. Her five daughters and one son were all together for the day supporting their friends wholeheartedly. Henry insisted on catering since he'd been in the middle of the Scottish charade that brought Ben and Cassidy together. He told her parents, who flew in from some place up north, that it was the least he could do for Cassidy since she saved his business from being torn apart by the likes of a Scot. One of the Murdock sisters caught the bouquet, but Ben's money was on Bolton being the next to marry after catching the garter belt, what with the exchange he saw between Bolton and Angel when no one was looking. Sadly, no one saw Charlie Knight in the mix. But that was to be expected until Ben let the poor man work on his new truck someday. The best part of the reception was when Christy's water broke. Once again, his friends all rushed to the hospital to greet a new member of their heart-filled southern family.

And so Benjamin and Cassidy Murray lived happily ever after. Of course, Ben handed over all of his money for Cassidy to multiply with her fancy investment skills, which precipitated a vastly better life. And that was a good thing, since he planned on having a whole mess of kids for them to spoil rotten with their love.

~ THE END ~

REMEMBERING SKYLINE

Thank you to my readers!
I am grateful to you for taking the time to purchase and read REMEMBERING SKYLINE. If you enjoyed this book, please leave a review at any retailer or on Goodreads.
Other titles in the SKYLINE MOUNTAIN series can be found on Amazon. All titles will be available at major retailers, soon.
I love hearing from readers and fans! Please stay in touch with me via the links below. And be sure to watch for more titles coming your way soon.

Facebook: Lesia Flynn Author Page
Twitter: @LesiaFlynn
Website: LesiaFlynn.com

Coming soon!
The last book in the Skyline Mountain Series
SKYLINE RESCUE
featuring Bolton and Angel
You won't want to miss their story of putting the past behind
and rediscovering who they really are.

Shop now at Amazon**!**

About the Author

Lesia Flynn is a native of Louisiana. She studied graphic design at LA Tech University. She lives in northern Alabama with her husband, children, and a rescue cat who is determined to save her from life's daily mishaps. She enjoys reading, writing, music, and art, but most of all, anything that provides an adventure! She loves hearing from fans. Please follow the link below to connect with her.

www.LesiaFlynn.com

Unlikely Rebel

Book One of
THE DARK REVOLUTION

AMY
BOYLES

Amy Boyles

Unlikely Rebel
by Amy Boyles

Copyright © 2015 Amy Boyles

*For Mark, for believing in me
when I didn't.*

CHAPTER ONE

I loved him the moment his dark eyes met mine, and I swore I would do anything to get him.

The year was 2087, the height of the second Civil War. The Patriot Party waged a fiery assault against the government in response to the oil drought. They were successful, winning cities and territories, burning as they went. I was nine. We lived in the city then and though there's not much I remember about that time, I do remember one night, the night I first laid eyes on Branthe.

Pop worked on unloading a wooden cart of food. It was a small load, some potatoes and apples, but if cooked right, it would last weeks. Mom sent me out to help him. I hung a lantern on the peg outside our door and raised the wick. The dismal amount of oil we could afford barely lit up half the cart.

I heard something down the street. A quick look revealed three men making their way toward us. Carrying sticks that they twirled like canes, the trio moved slowly, as if measuring up a man and his daughter.

"Hurry, Anna," he said.

The first one, his cane twirling, twirling, twirling, said, "Unloading some supplies, are you? Looks like a nice amount of food. Looks like it could feed us for maybe a night. Maybe two."

"Yeah, we could use a good meal," another added.

"Maybe we could use a girl, too."

The trio laughed.

"Go inside," Pop commanded quietly as the men sauntered up.

I moved to obey but a hand snatched my collar. A gruff voice whispered in my ear, "Where are you going, little one?"

I heard something as my legs pumped desperately forward. It sounded like feet scuffing against rock, like a stick hitting something dull and like my father huffing and moaning. As I tried to move forward, the hand dragged me back.

"Leave her be!" Pop snarled. I turned and saw it then, the blood running down his leg. With a blade stuck in his calf and the flesh torn, the crimson trickle made its way to his ankle.

Then he appeared. Out from the shadows he stepped, tall and lean with broad shoulders and eyes as dark as ink. Rebel and wanton, gentleman and rogue, traitor and fighter, people whispered that he was death and life itself. Hero and villain, lover and hater, he exemplified what every man wanted to be and what every woman simply wanted. The man stepped into the feeble pool of light provided by our lantern, the illumination pallid compared to his presence. Even the lantern seemed to shake, quaking before him.

"Release them and I'll let you live," he stated simply.

They laughed as bad men are wont to do. A knife flashed a silvery reflection as it moved toward my father's middle. Before the shriek of horror in the back of my throat left my mouth, the stranger twisted the man's wrist, took the knife and gutted him. In three quick flashes, the rest of the men were laid out, howling and crying for mercy.

There was none. The stranger sliced each of their throats to silence them. It was no less than they would've done to my father. I felt no pity for them.

"Are you all right?" he asked.

"Yes," Pop said, studying the wound. "It's not deep. I can clean and sew it. It'll be fine. Please, take some food for your help."

He shook his head. My eyes washed over him, stopping at his long hair. Securely pulled back in the new style of the queue, the tip of it curled under. I wanted to pull it, but that was silly.

"I didn't do this for food." He picked me up and sat me on his knee. "And how are you, little one?"

I rested close enough to touch his face. The tan skin angled sharply at the jaw. A bit of beard sprouted from his chin, making him appear rough, yet his eyes sparkled when they looked at me. It was the handsomest face I'd ever seen.

"Fine," I whispered.

"And so you are," he said, putting me down. He stepped into the shadows of the house and disappeared.

"Thank you, Branthe," Pop whispered.

Branthe. From that day on, the name was burned into my memory. For in the moment when he saved our lives, I loved him and would never love anyone else.

CHAPTER TWO

Ten years passed before I saw him again.

With the war long finished and the Patriot Party in power, things were different. You could ask almost anyone, and though they wouldn't tell you the truth for fear of retribution in the form of imprisonment or slavery, the word *patriot* was a hoax.

The new government used the term because of the revolution of 1776. They saw themselves as setting the country to right, destroying much of the technology that poisoned our water and air, even going so far as mandating that everyone dress from the era. Personally, I hated it, despising the plain linen and scratchy muslin. I especially hated corsets because they were so ridiculously tight. It certainly wasn't a woman who demanded all those of the female gender burn their bras and don a wardrobe that was three hundred years old.

But I digress...

What food couldn't be cultivated required purchasing and money didn't grow anywhere, much less on trees. Mom mended and washed for rich ladies while Pop worked as a carpenter.

My brother, Colvin, left a couple years earlier to become a journeyman to a blacksmith. A blacksmith, of all things. It was a word I thought I'd only ever read in books.

That left me.

"Going to go check the traps, are you, Anna?" old Mrs. Sims asked while scouring an iron pot.

I nodded, stealing a bit of bacon left over from the colonel's breakfast. "I plan on it."

She smacked my hand. "Better not steal from the master's plate. You know what he's like."

"Ouch," I replied in mock pain. "What he doesn't know, won't hurt me," I joked.

Gray wisps of hair poked out from beneath her bonnet. With a pudgy finger, she set them to right. "Don't be smart. Men in charge of prisons aren't known to be the most merciful. Be careful there, girl. Besides, I need the candlesticks from his room to clean. They're tarnished."

I looked out the kitchen window for his carriage. "Is he gone?"

She eyed me. "Would I send you up there if I knew he was here? He's gone. He left a little while ago for the prison. It should be safe."

Shoving the last morsel of bacon in my mouth, I wiped my hands on a mostly clean towel. "I'll be back and then I'm going to check the traps."

I took the back stairs two at a time, each one creaking under my weight. Before the colonel was assigned the old plantation house, it had been a historic site. There were front stairs and back stairs, servants' quarters and main rooms.

In all, the mansion oozed grandiosity, being much too large for a single man and his household.

I found myself whistling a nonsensical tune as I approached the bedroom. Once this was done, I would be out the door and looking for snared rabbits for the rest of the afternoon. That being one of the few things I looked forward to between work and home, I wanted to put this task behind me and get moving.

The door opened with an eerie creak. A quick scan of the room revealed the candlesticks on the mahogany desk, exactly where they always were. Picking them up, I spied a letter.

Curiosity getting the better of me, I snuck a quick peak. Penned from someone named Lord Andrews, it was an invitation for the colonel to stay in his mansion in Corinth. I smirked. Good. Maybe the colonel would go and never return.

The door groaned shut. I turned to see the figure of Colonel Mann, the warden who wasn't supposed to be there, the man Mrs. Sims promised she'd seen leaving only a few minutes earlier, standing with his prominent backside against the wall.

"Anna, I didn't expect to see you."

I curtsied, as was proper, though I hated every moment of the action. "Mrs. Sims needs to clean the candlesticks. She sent me to get them for her."

He raised an eyebrow over his acne-scarred face. Plump cheeks puffed out, half hiding his beady eyes. The small mouth puckered like a fish in dire need of water, and his tongue slithered over his lips like a snake tasting the air. His features were repugnant on a good day and hideous on all others.

He took a step toward me. "I don't think she'll be needing those immediately, do you?"

I shifted one leg forward to pass him but he blocked me. For a fat man, the colonel could move. "She will miss them *and* me if I'm not in the kitchen in a moment or two."

He took them from my hands. "I disagree."

A cold tingle pulsed through my body. Mrs. Sims had set me up. She knew what he wanted and had willingly delivered me right into his rotund arms.

He licked his lips. "I know how you like to run away from me. That may be hard to do now."

Chin raised, I did my best not to let him see the fear that had taken hold of me. The colonel wasn't known as a nice or even fair man. "I just...I have a lot of work to do. Is there something you need from me?"

He stroked one of the candlesticks. "You, my dear. Very simply put. You. Tell me, Anna, have you been rendered? It's past time if it hasn't happened. After all, you're well past the age of marriage. It seems a girl as pretty as you should've gone through the ritual already. But if you haven't, we can do it now and I'll be sure to write up an official report."

Rendered. At the sound of the word, a metallic taste filled my mouth. "I've gone through the ritual and was found to be whole." It was a lie but if I said anything else, he'd have me flat on the desk and my skirts up checking for himself.

"Oh, well then," he said, taking another step toward me, "I know it's important to keep you wholesome. I can do that. We can play and I can keep you intact." His fingers ran up my arm. "Would you like that?"

It was rumored that he tortured the prisoners, that in his office sat a cabinet full of knives and whips. I didn't need to give him a reason to put me in that place and do whatever he wished to me. Here, I was safe. Or, safer than I would be locked up.

"I...I must save myself."

He laughed. "Come now, you can still save yourself. As I said, there are ways to keep you intact." He stopped and then added, "I know you've been stealing from me."

"I don't know what you mean."

"You've been taking a rabbit here and there home with you. I don't blame you. People are hungry. But when you take, you must give."

He dropped the candlesticks and pulled up my skirt. His fingers brushed my thighs, their touch rough and unkind. He felt the round curve of my buttocks, squeezing the flesh. His touch stunned me so much that I didn't think to protest. Until I felt his mouth on mine. I pushed him away but he held fast.

A knock on the door. "Master, are you in there?" Richmond, the butler.

"No," he fumed, breaking from me.

It was all I needed. With the surprise interruption, his hands dropped. I wiggled from him, grabbed the candlesticks and said, "I must take these to Mrs. Sims."

I opened the door to find Richmond. He gave me a knowing nod that told me he'd come to my rescue. He then entered the room to speak to the colonel. With my back against one of the walls in the hallway, I collected myself. I tucked my hands under my arms to keep them from shaking and took several deep breaths.

I decided then and there that no matter how good the money, my time with the colonel was finished. I tightened my grip around the candlesticks and proceeded to take them to Mrs. Sims. After that, I would check the traps for rabbits, because if there was anything I deserved from the bastard, it was a good meal.

CHAPTER THREE

I'd set five snares on the land behind the mansion. The tract normally yielded a good catch as the twenty thousand or so acres used to be a national forest. But that was when the state controlled the region, before the Patriot government declared all lands belonged to them. Still, the area delivered good food, my main concern. With some luck, all the traps would be full. It would be a nice going-away present from the colonel.

I knew the terrain well. My family's parcel of property sat only a half-mile away, so I'd been exploring the woods for years. Reaching a bluff, I walked the ledge until I came to a sharp divide in the rocks. Built like a small ravine in the stone, I sat down, wedging myself between the two peaks. I'd slid down it a thousand times, but this time, maybe because the encounter with Mann distracted me, I forgot to tuck the fabric of my dress under my arm. The hem snagged and ripped, creating a long gash up the thigh.

"Dammit to hell," I swore. A quick inspection revealed one torn skirt and a dirty petticoat, which equaled an hour's worth of hemming when I got home. Not how I wanted to spend any of my time.

The rest of the way proved clear. The leaves were turning, and as such, many had left their homes among the trees to blanket the ground in gold and orange. Looking at them gave me some peace, which I needed. With my spirits lifted, something akin to happiness filled my heart.

Then I came to the first snare. Empty. Disappointed but not dejected, I moved on to the next one. There, I had better luck. Caught in the noose of the trap hung a hare. Swinging peacefully in the forest breeze with a broken neck, the animal was quite dead. I unhinged it from the snare and traveled on. The next trap sat empty as well. That only left two more.

The fourth lay behind a thicket of cedars whose branches hung low to the ground. I pushed the spiny green arms back only to find a knife blade at my throat.

"Who are you?" came the gruff voice.

Four men stood before me, all the worse for the rags they wore. The voice in question came from the one with the blade. He was older, balding, with a scraggly beard. His government-rationed waistcoat and breeches were muddy and torn, and the linen cravat at his throat held a sweat ring that looked to go clear around his neck. One thing was certain — they were rebels, a group of citizens stuck squarely in the middle, not siding with either the patriots or the original government. When the patriots won, their side lost, making them criminals against the government. These men had probably been in hiding since the end of the war. They definitely smelled like it.

"Who are you?" he repeated.

"My name's Anna."

The men looked behind them to a thick cedar. Slowly, the branches pushed away and another emerged. Tall with broad shoulders, his every movement embodied the words *lithe* and *muscular*, for he moved with the fluidity of water and the strength of a bull. His dark eyes flashed an intelligence that made me cower yet yearn for him simultaneously. His clothes, government rationed though they were, accentuated his muscular thighs and forearms, as if forcing me to acknowledge I stood in the presence of not only a man, but a remarkable creation.

There was no doubt in my mind who he was.

"What are you doing here, Anna?" he asked lightly, as if his man wasn't holding a blade to my throat.

Though part of me wanted to stand there for eternity and bathe in the sight of him, I managed to find my tongue. "I'm collecting the rabbits in my snares. Please release your hound from me so that I may leave." I didn't say I planned to be nice.

He pulled two rabbits from his pouch. "You mean you're the one who caught these?"

Extending an open palm, I retorted, "I'll thank you kindly to give me my catch so that I can leave you men to your business."

They laughed. Not the reaction I'd hoped for.

Branthe tossed one of the rabbits to me. "My men are hungry. It wouldn't do me any good to starve them. I hope you don't mind if we keep one of your claims."

"Thank you."

"But you realize I can't let you leave."

I looked in those piercing dark eyes of his. They were mesmerizing, bewitching me so that I couldn't look away. When I finally forced my gaze to the ground, I did so knowing the truth. He wasn't going to release me.

Having waited so long to be near this man, it seemed contradictory but I didn't want to run off with him. I didn't want to be anyone's prisoner. Times were dangerous, from both the rebel and patriot sides.

I tried again. "My family isn't political. I hold no ambitions of rising through the party. I don't have any reason to betray you."

He offered a sad smile. "I can't let you go. Fief, lower your blade and check to make sure she's unarmed. After that, tie her up." His eyes flickered back to mine. "The rabbit I gave you is your dinner. Be thankful for it. You'll be eating better than the rest of us tonight. I won't be able to promise such luxuries in the future."

I broke free of Fief. What a stupid name. "You saved us once. When I was young, you saved my father from a gang of men who attacked him."

He paused, taking me in for what seemed forever. "And?"

It felt like my chest caved in. For ten years I'd dreamed of this day and all he had to say when I told him I admired him, no *revered* him, was *And*?

"That may not mean anything to you, but it means something to me. I'm loyal to your cause. I won't betray you, not to anyone. Please. Let me go. My family needs this food."

I eyed a dagger at the waist of one of the men. If I moved a few more inches to the left it would be within reach. And I'd still be surrounded by five armed men. It was a foolish thought.

Branthe watched my eyes travel to the weapon and back. "You're going with us and it's in your best interest not to do anything rash. I can promise you protection. But if you act out, I can promise you nothing. Now, which would you rather have — protection or nothing?"

At first, I didn't understand. Then I glanced at his men. Though they didn't accost me with seedy looks, it was obvious what he meant.

There was no other choice. "Protection," I murmured.

"Then tie her up," he commanded.

CHAPTER FOUR

It didn't take long for them to discover the jackrabbit in my pack and confiscate it. Not that it mattered. They would've sniffed it out sooner or later and by that time the meat would've turned, making it inedible for all.

We walked south for perhaps a mile or two. The choice of direction was curious as nothing significant lay that way. If anything, our travels only led deeper into the woods. Which, if you were a band of rebels wanting to avoid detection, was the best direction to go.

By late afternoon, the men made a small campfire, just enough to warm us and cook the meat. Branthe positioned himself by me, though he said not a word. The scent of leather and dried leaves wafted off him.

A few times I snuck side glances at him. He appeared to always be looking forward, scanning the woods as if waiting for something to jump out and attack. His shoulders were pulled back and tense, always waiting.

"Thank you for sharing your dinner."

Pressing my forehead against a shoulder, I attempted to get a piece of rogue hair out of my eyes. It didn't work. "You're kidding, right? It's not like I had a choice."

He smirked. His penetrating gaze made me feel as if the man saw directly into my soul. Enchanted and unnerved, I looked away, knowing that if I spent too much time within the grasp of his glance, I would be seduced. And I refused to be prisoner as well as mistress.

He leaned back, stretching his taut body across a bed of leaves. Propping himself on an elbow, he said, "I'm attempting to be nice, or cordial as the government would have us say. You don't have to accept my gratitude, but it would be appreciated."

I tried blowing the strand from my face. That didn't work, either. "Well maybe if you let me go, I would accept your thanks."

"You know I can't do that."

"No. I know you can, but you won't."

"So you won't accept my thanks." Those eyes swept over me from head to foot. Whenever Colonel Mann looked at me that way I felt dirty and needed a bath immediately afterwards. This felt different. He sized me up – not as adversary or ally, but simply as me.

"Trying to decide how much of a threat I am?"

"I don't think you're a threat."

I didn't know if I should be insulted or relieved by his assessment. "Then what are you doing?"

"I was admiring your hair."

"My hair?" I asked, disbelief evident in my voice.

"The way the light reflects off it gives it a hint of red. It's lovely."

Who was this man? I knew his aim wasn't to charm me. He didn't seem the type. Yet there was something honest and reflective in his tone that caused my heart to beat faster.

So instead of taking the compliment like a lady would have, I replied, "You say that to all the girls."

"Do you see any other girls?" He paused, glancing over at his men. "You know, it's very difficult to have a conversation with someone who can't accept a compliment."

This line of conversation needed to stop. He was confident, engaging, mesmerizing – all the things I knew he would be and all the things I wanted from a man. Superficially, of course. On a deeper level, I wanted kindness and generosity – traits I already knew he possessed.

For goodness' sake, the man was seduction on a stick. For too long I had yearned for Branthe. I wouldn't be seduced and tossed away like a streetwalker. So instead of replying, I blew on my face, but that damned hair still didn't move.

"You have a piece of hair stuck to your face."

"I know that! It's driving me almost as crazy as you."

He laughed, the corners of his eyes crinkling in sort of a magical way. It annoyed me.

"If I remove it, will you accept my thanks?"

"I'll think about it."

His dark eyes held mine as he lifted a hand. With a gentle yet even stroke, he picked the hair from my face and tucked it behind an ear. The electric touch of his fingers sent a shiver down my spine. I licked my lips in an attempt to distract my thoughts. More nervous habit than anything else, I didn't expect him to notice, but his gaze followed my tongue. Hot flames licked my cheeks as a blush washed over me.

"Thank you," I murmured.

"No. Thank you," he said and without another word, Branthe left my presence to join his men.

He didn't talk to me again that day, though he made certain his men untied me for dinner. Once everyone finished eating, I found myself bound again for the long night ahead. Worse, they wrapped the rope around a tree, ensuring I couldn't escape. I spent that night waking every few minutes in pain from the ache in my back and shoulders.

The next morning we set out early. Once again I didn't know our destination, but wherever it resided, we were definitely going in the wrong direction.

"You don't want to go that way," I said sharply. They spoke little, which made me think my words and tone needed to be dramatic. Other than Branthe, they didn't appear very educated. I didn't even know if most of them spoke English.

The one called Fief snarled at me. "Why not?"

"Because that way the forest gets swampy. Though autumn is coming, the days are still warm, and most likely so is the water."

"Meaning?" He asked with impatience.

I sighed. Really? Didn't they know where they were? "Meaning - water moccasins. I don't suppose you possess anti-venom in those packs of yours, do you? I mean, you had to steal my family's supper so I seriously doubt it."

The look he gave me was pure agitation. "What do you think, boss?"

Branthe crossed his arms and strode over to me. One, two, three long-legged strides and he stood within six inches of my face. I sucked in my breath. It appeared the simple act of him putting one foot in front of the other, otherwise known as walking, took the air from me. This close, I noticed his brown eyes were flecked with gold and green. I gulped as he studied my face.

"What of that way?" he asked, pointing east.

I shrugged. "That's the way you should go. I don't know where you're headed, but that way is the safer route of the two."

The men looked back and forth at each other, shifting their weight from hip to hip.

"I say she's lying," Fief, the apparent second in command, blurted out. "Could be a trap. Send us toward people she knows, hoping we'll be overpowered and taken."

I felt Branthe's probing eyes once more. I stared defiantly at him, waiting for his grand judgment.

"I have no intention of being bitten by a snake. It's not a trap, it's purely self-preservation. But don't listen to me, I only grew up around here."

His eyes flickered from me to his men. At last, he spoke. "We keep moving in the same direction."

"Then let me tie my skirts. I'm not going to ruin this dress anymore than I already have." I eyed the gash up the side. Plodding through brush and over rocks had made it worse. It now needed at least two hours of mending to redeem it.

I fiddled with my skirt for a lot longer than necessary, annoying them on purpose. Finally, I finished and we moved on. It wasn't an hour later that we hit the first of the stagnant water. No one said anything. They just waded through the murky pools of blackness, staying to the outer edge as much as possible. After we'd been at it for nearly half the day, I said something.

"If you travel west, the water will let up in time to camp for the night."

This time, Branthe didn't stop to study my facial expression. "Do it," he agreed.

How epic of him to realize I wasn't lying. After shucking my water-filled boots through the swamp for another hour, we hit dry land. The men looked as tired as I felt. They collapsed on the ground, peeling off boots and wringing out socks.

There was no food that night and the fire was put out well before dark. I sat, wrists tied, leaning against a tree. The men made no move to talk to me. It was just as well, I didn't have anything to say. As the sun sank toward the horizon, he sat down next to me.

"So you didn't lie to us," Branthe said casually.

"No," I confirmed.

"Why not?"

I gave him a look that conveyed, *do I look stupid* but simply replied, "I told you before, I'm not a patriot any more than you are. All I want is to go home."

Though he eyed me with skepticism, he only remarked, "Fair enough."

"So will you let me?"

"No," he stated. "If you hadn't seen us, we wouldn't be in this situation. But you did and that changed things."

"Who are you?" I asked, raising an eyebrow. Part of me hoped he would give the answer I knew to be true. "You know my name. It's only fair that I know my captor's."

"Some names are better left unsaid."

"Only names that carry great weight can't be spoken."

He stared at me in a way that made goose bumps rise on my flesh. "More than you know."

"And what if I wanted to know?"

"It's too much responsibility for a girl we kidnapped in the forest."

"And if I want the responsibility? After all, I have pretty hair. Doesn't that count for something?"

His mouth quirked into a smile. "No need to remind me. Your hair has been blinding me all day."

"Has it really?"

"No," he said tersely. But then he smiled. My heart melted, pooling at my feet.

He continued on. "Anyway, no one's ever wanted that responsibility before."

"I find that hard to believe."

"Why? Being a rebel isn't an easy life."

"But surely there are others who want to help you, who've given themselves to your cause." I didn't want to say what I thought – that there were plenty of women who would gladly give themselves to him in exchange for his heart and his trust.

Picking up a leaf, he twirled it between two fingers. "I have to think about it. I need to know if you're worthy of the information. What can you offer in exchange?"

I didn't know if he meant physically or metaphorically, so I decided to play it safe. "Nothing. I can offer you nothing but my trust and loyalty. As I said, you once saved my father's life and mine. I already owe you. Knowing your name will only mean that my trust rests with the right man."

He touched my wrist, pushing away the ropes and rubbing the welts that had formed over the past couple of days. His fingers stroked the burns with gentleness, as if he felt the discomfort they caused me. A wave of energy soared through me. No one's touch had ever elicited that response from my body. I felt tied to him, tethered by his touch.

He looked up, his doe-bright eyes full of something akin to sadness. "How can you be so sure the person who saved you was me?"

I smiled. "I would know you in my sleep."

He smiled but said nothing. We sat in silence as he pulled a tin of balm from a pack and applied it to my wrists. They were instantly soothed. I thanked him but he remained quiet.

"So is your new plan to torture me with your silence?"

He laughed. "You were so pleasant when you thanked me. But now the moment is gone. Do you think my company so vile?"

I gave him a hard stare. "I am your prisoner, after all."

"Would you rather be in a patriot prison? From the looks of those rabbits you stole from Colonel Mann, you would be sitting in his facility right now if we hadn't rescued you."

I yanked my wrists back into my lap and retorted, "Rescued me? You've done nothing but make my plight worse. And what makes you think those were his rabbits?"

He gave me a knowing look. "The traps were set behind his property. It doesn't take a genius to figure that out."

"I'd take anything other than this," I grumbled.

His dark eyes seared into me. "Spend one night in a patriot prison and you'll change your mind."

"Can't be any worse than here," I said snidely.

"Ask any of my men. Beaten for no reason and whipped for less. The food was piss and feces. Most of them only survived by killing rats. The reds say they want to help people, but they're less than human."

"And I still haven't figured out which category you fall into," I fumed.

His eyes narrowed and then he turned to his second. "Fief, tell young Anna why you were imprisoned."

The man snorted. "I fixed a mechanical cart for an old man. He paid me in apples. A nearby soldier saw it and accused him of giving away his fair share of government rations."

"So then it was his fault."

He nodded. "Yes, they wanted to arrest him but I told them I would take his punishment. He was old, and wouldn't have survived in prison. For taking his place, I think they made it worse. These aren't people. They aren't fit to be our leaders and yet they won and here we are."

"So then how did you escape?"

Before he could answer, a troupe of Patriots clad in red — we called them *reds*, for red, white and blue — burst through the forest. There was no pause for questions. The men pulled their swords and pistols and started swinging and firing.

The rope around my wrists fell away. Branthe leaned into my ear and said one word.

"Run."

I didn't have to be told twice. The rogues threw themselves on the reds, giving me an easy chance to slip away. I gave one last look back at Branthe, whose short sword tangled with one of the redcoats. It was too early to see who would win and I didn't have time to watch.

Running as fast as my legs could pump, I cleared small ravines, jumped over creeks and bounded up rocks as fast as possible. I didn't stop until it was pitch black and I couldn't see a tree branch in front of my face.

Exhausted and blinded, I put my head down on the forest floor and slept.

CHAPTER FIVE

"Anna."

The voice was neither foreign nor welcome. In the place between dreams and wakefulness, I tried to place it. The name and face didn't come.

The voice gently shook my shoulder. "Anna, it's time to wake up."

I bolted straight up. When I opened my eyes, the face staring back at me was who I feared.

"Mann," I whispered.

"You slept so long I didn't think you'd recognize me when you woke up."

My tone was sharper than I intended. "How could I not?"

"Tsk. Tsk. Is that any way to thank the man who saved you?"

My mind raced. Saved me from what? Last I remembered I had fallen asleep on the forest floor. "I don't remember you saving me."

His lips puckered up, accentuating the lines and pocks around his mouth. "Then you must not have seen the rebels. It's amazing that you didn't, seeing how the patriot scouts found them so near you and how they said a young woman had been with them. Unfortunately, the men escaped my scouts, but it seems I've found a young woman as substitute."

"I was out looking for rabbits." The lie lived beyond the edge of terrible, dwelling in the abysmal. He wouldn't believe it, but it was all I had. "I got lost. I couldn't remember where a couple of the snares were and ended up deep in the woods."

The fat bastard leered. "But you grew up near those woods. It must've been a good hiding spot where you set that snare."

"It was."

He stood up and lit a candle. Though a few sconces lined the walls, I hadn't noticed my surroundings or been able to, actually, since his round face took up all of my view. But now I saw gray walls, an oval-shaped desk and a wooden cabinet. The cabinet caught my attention. Drawers lined one side while the other held a single door. Rumors of torture tools flooded my mind.

"Do you like my office? When I first received the post as warden, I wasn't too happy with it. I thought it drab. But I have to say, it's grown on me."

"Where am I?" I asked, dread filling me.

"You haven't guessed? You're at Bolden Prison, my home away from home."

"What am I doing here?" I did my best to keep my voice even, but knew I fell short.

Colonel Mann flipped up the tail of his coat and sat down on a wooden bench. He eyed me with curiosity as if genuinely surprised by my question.

"You know, Anna, I wanted to make this easy for you, I really did. I didn't want it to be a struggle or something you didn't want, but after what happened a few days ago, I realized it would be both. Knowing you'd never consent willingly to be with me, I decided that force would be the only way to take you.

"My initial plan was to wait until you returned the next day. But as you know, you never came to work." He adjusted the crotch of his breeches and settled back onto the bench. "At that point, I thought I'd missed my chance. There'd be no way to take you, is what I thought. But then something rather intriguing happened. You landed in my lap, surfacing near the spot where known criminals had just been."

He leaned forward and licked his lips. "So you see, you're here because I have a strong suspicion you know exactly who those men were and I plan on finding out."

He pulled back the blanket that covered me. I lay atop a metal table. A leather strap was fitted over my waist and attached to another strap, securing me tightly. My legs were parted and also strapped down. I was, for all intents and purposes, not going anywhere.

He pulled a black leather glove off his right hand. "Now, I believe we left off when I was just about to find out whether or not you're a virgin."

CHAPTER SIX

A knock sounded. "Forever to be interrupted by someone," Mann grumbled. He patted my leg. "Don't worry. Whatever it is, it won't keep me from you for very long. I promise."

With a heavy sigh and even heavier gate, he crossed to the door and opened it. "What do you want?" he demanded of the man in red on the other side.

"Sir, there's a problem with some prisoners in cell block A."

"Then deal with it," he snapped.

The man looked down, embarrassed. "We're trying to. The men are asking for you. They think your presence will help."

He tightened his belt. "How bad is it?"

"They have a guard."

Mann blanched and without a word to me, left. I sighed. Safe for now, but how long? I wriggled against the straps. They were tight. Dammit. I kept squirming though, hoping at some point they would come loose. It occurred to me that even if I got out of my binds, how would I escape? I focused on trying to create a rudimentary plan. Fixated on this, I didn't hear two more guards enter.

"There she is," said one red to another. "What is it the colonel wants done with her again?"

The second man, hat pulled down to his eyes, replied, "He wants her escorted to the mansion."

It was worse than I thought. There would be no safe haven for me, no way to escape.

The first guard pulled his pistol and focused it on me. "No sudden moves."

I obeyed, allowing the second man to untie all my bindings and waited while he tied my wrists together. He pulled me to a standing position and shoved me toward the door. "Get on with you."

He led me through the cavernous prison. At one time, when there was still electricity, it probably had been ablaze with light. Now, it was a dark husk of a building, dank and cold. I was glad to be leaving it.

It didn't take long to reach the outer door. There, the first guard left us. We walked across the lawn and met a horse-drawn cart. At the front of it sat a man with broad shoulders. I thought I recognized him from behind, but I didn't want to get my hopes up. After all, the past two days had been anything but fantastic.

The guard placed me in the cart and sat down beside me. Once we were clear of the gate, he handed me a flask and bread. "Eat up," he said. "We've a long journey in front of us."

Startled, I replied, "So you're not taking me to the mansion?"

The man driving turned around. It was Branthe! He smiled at the man beside me. "I guess you did your job all too well, Fief. She didn't even recognize you."

"Have you rescued me only to capture me again? If that's the case, you can take me back to Colonel Mann."

"Don't worry, Anna. We're taking you someplace safe. Or, as safe as you can be since you're now a wanted woman."

"Wanted?"

He tipped his tricorn hat to me. "Stay around rogues and rebels long enough and you'll be considered one. I'm afraid that's the fate you've found for yourself."

I crossed my arms. "Are there any other choices?"

"You've seen our faces. I could have you killed." My expression must've revealed my fear because he added, "Don't worry. I'm only joking. Now eat some food. Fief was right, we have a long way in front of us."

CHAPTER SEVEN

"You can never return home."

I awoke in what was left of the city of Corinth. Before the war, the city existed in a state known as Tennessee. Now, it simply resided in the United States, Southern Quadrant.

The home belonged to a family who also had one daughter. She'd brought me meat (what kind was questionable) and water while I slept in what was probably her bed, regaining my strength. But now Branthe, the man who refused to acknowledge his name, presumed to tell me things he knew nothing about.

With both hands behind his back, he looked out the window. His voice was calm, steady, and the complete opposite of mine. "Corinth is now your home. Forget about where you came from."

"What of my parents? If Mann wants me, won't they be in danger?"

"They've already been sent for."

"What?" I asked, surprised.

He spun toward me. His glance immediately turned my knees to rubber. Those dark eyes of his softened, as if he regretted that any of this had happened. Well he should, all of it was his damn fault.

"Sit down and I'll tell you everything."

"Including your name?"

His eyes lighted for a moment and then the curl of a smile tugged at one corner of his lips. "If you wish to know. It's as much as you deserve."

I sat on the lumpy bed with a huff. "I should think so since I'm now a wanted fugitive, thanks to you and your men. But first, I want to know how you found me."

He took off his coat, revealing a much nicer waistcoat than I expected. It was silk embroidered damask, and was both elegant and beautiful. The light sage color offset his tanned skin and highlighted the green flecks in his eyes. He then rolled his shirtsleeves back. The muscles of his forearms popped in an homage to masculinity. My mouth watered. I swallowed, trying not to choke on saliva.

"After the skirmish, I sent Fief out to follow you. He saw by your tracks that you'd been taken. It wasn't hard to figure out where to. I knew Mann would quickly realize you were with us. He'll do anything to get information on me and my men. And when I say anything, I mean it. There was no choice but to go after you and to be honest, in some ways this solved my problem of what to do with you."

I bit the inside of my lip. He made it sound like I was a stray dog he was deciding whether or not to neuter. "What to do with me?"

"I couldn't immediately release you because Mann would question you regarding those missing rabbits. It's a crime to steal food, in case you've forgotten."

I shook my head in annoyance. "I already had a plan for that."

He looked at me with amusement. "Which was?"

"To tell him the traps were empty."

He laughed softly. "I don't think it would've worked. He's not stupid. Anyway, my plan was to keep you with us for a few days, just long enough for the initial heat of your disappearance to cool down."

My head swam. "So you were going to release me?"

He nodded. "But first my men and I needed to put some distance between us and the area where you lived. It was always my plan."

I shook my head in disgust. "Why didn't you just tell me that?"

He sighed, propping one leg atop the seat of a wooden chair. "Because I didn't want you to like us. In my business, I don't make it a habit of forming friends. I'm not the sort of companion you want to have."

"So you were pushing me away when you rubbed ointment on my wrists?"

His eyes hardened. "Your wounds didn't need to get infected."

Keep telling yourself that. "Your name," I commanded, closing the distance between us.

He pushed a strand of hair away from my ear. His fingers slid down my neck, stopping at the top of my shoulder. He leaned over, his breath hot as it cascaded from my ear down to my neck.

"Don't you already know my name?"

My hands trembled. One more inch and his lips would be on my skin. And I wanted it. Oh, how I wanted it. "I need to hear you say it."

He pulled back, studying me for a long moment as if searching my soul for something, as if deciding if I was worthy of knowing the truth of his identity.

"You'll be disappointed."

"I doubt it."

"I'm—"

The door burst open. A young man with a mop of blond hair sauntered into the room. It had been too long since I'd seen him. "They've arrived safely," he said.

"Colvin," I gasped. "What are you doing here?"

My brother swept me into his arms. "I learned what happened and came to escort Mom and Pop to the city before the reds came for them."

"But how did you know? Aren't you working for a blacksmith?"

He gave Branthe a knowing look. My eyes shifted between them until the realization of what was going on stepped on my toe. "You work for him? But I thought—"

He stroked my hair like our mother would've done if she'd been there. "It was a necessary lie. One to keep you safe. We're no better off than we were before the war. In fact, things are worse. I couldn't sit by and watch my family starve."

It took me a moment to absorb what he was saying. So everything he'd told me about leaving to find work was a lie. At any point, he could've been killed and I never would've known. Along with everything else that had happened in the last couple of days, this was almost too much. I wiped a budding tear from under my eye.

"Where are they?"

"They're in a safe house not far from here. I'll take you to them."

"Please," I replied. I turned to say something to Branthe, but he was gone. He couldn't have left the way Colvin entered, because he would've crossed my line of sight. For some reason, I hadn't noticed it before, but there was an open window facing the alley behind us. Wind blew the sheer curtain inward. Smiling to myself, I realized he'd left the exact same way he had all those years ago when he saved my father's life.

He vanished.

CHAPTER EIGHT

Corinth was a cesspool of filth and trash. With no electricity, the sewers no longer worked. Though it reeked as if sewage should be careening down the roads, it wasn't. But it still smelled that way. The stench assaulted me, halting any forward progress my legs tried to make. Colvin handed me a cloth.

"Cover your nose. It helps."

The creamy muslin smelled of lavender and spearmint. Like a weird sort of chewing gum that I wouldn't want to eat.

"It's what they used to do in the cities."

"Like when?"

"A long time ago. A few centuries."

"Well, good to know."

We passed other men and women in the streets. All of them wore standard issue clothing, looking like copies of one another. We'd lived in the country for so long, it didn't occur to me that in some places everyone was dressed the exact same way. It was frightening, reminding me of how much control the reds possessed. This was no longer a free country and hadn't been for a long time.

"How long have you worked for—"

"Shh. Don't say his name. Never say his name. There are ears everywhere and those ears have blades."

We turned down what looked to be an ancient stone path. Three houses down was a small brick cottage. Soot stained, it didn't look like much, but when my brother opened the door, it held my world.

"Mom! Pop!" I ran into their waiting arms.

"Anna, are you all right?" Pop asked.

"Couldn't be better," I said. Taking a moment to look around the house, I saw that it was small, with a wood stove positioned in what used to be the dining room. It was also dark. The tallow candles burning barely released enough light for me to see past the faces in the room.

I turned to Colvin. "How long do we have to stay here?"

He gave our father a knowing look. "There aren't any definites, but it will be a while."

Pop grasped my shoulders gently. "We've been given new papers so we have some freedom, but we'll never be able to go home. At this point, reds are watching the house and have probably paid off our friends to betray us if we return."

"Never go home?" I mumbled, sinking into a nearby chair. "Our lives gone?"

"Not gone," Mom said, rubbing my shoulder. "Different. We won't have to stay here forever, but until it's safe for us to leave for the country, this will be our new home."

Looking at their faces, I waited for the joke. I waited for one of them to crack a smile. It didn't happen.

The words erupted from my mouth in defiance. "So we're prisoners here?"

Colvin patted my head. "For now, but wouldn't you rather be rebel prisoners waiting to be released than a patriot prisoner, slowly starving in a cell?"

"I suppose so, but not that it's going to make a difference. A prisoner is a prisoner, no matter what." And so that's what I believed, hoping I wouldn't have to eat those words.

CHAPTER NINE

Later that night, as I brushed my hair before bedtime in a vain attempt to have some sort of normalcy in my newly upturned life, I thought I heard something outside my window. It sounded like pebbles or something stupid like that being thrown against it. Going to look, I peered through the smudged glass but saw nothing. Without any street lamps burning, the world was pitch black once the sun went down.

Cities were strange places. As soon as the sun passed twilight, everyone bolted for their homes. Houses became individual forts with steel bolts and wooden barricades locking doors up tightly. Inside shutters were closed and locked and everything was silent save for the crickets and occasional howl of a coyote.

Satisfied that nothing was outside, I blew out my candle and settled into bed. Exhausted from the day's events, I opened my eyes at the feel of a hand over my mouth.

"It's only me. Don't be afraid."

Branthe. What the hell was he doing here? And why the hell was he sneaking into my room at night? "Some might say I should be afraid, what with you sneaking in and all."

"Would you say that?"

"Maybe." After a long pause I added, "No."

The bed creaked as he sat down atop it. I bunched my knees under me and pushed myself up.

"What are you doing here? You left without a word earlier today."

"Yes," he said, as if remembering why he'd come, "I wanted to thank you."

"For what?"

"For not telling Colonel Mann anything about me or my men."

My body shivered at the name. I didn't like hearing it and hoped I'd be able to forget he ever existed soon enough.

"It's me who should be thanking you for rescuing me."

"See, not all rebels are bad."

"You mean, not all rebels are kidnappers?"

He laughed softly. "That too." He shifted on the bed, causing it to creak. I hoped my parents didn't hear. "Were you really going to thank me? It seems a tall task for someone as sassy as you."

"I'm not sassy," I argued.

"Of course not. Arguing with me like that definitely proves you have no sass."

I sighed. "Thank you for rescuing me."

"That was easy, wasn't it?"

"Don't worry, next time I won't thank you so readily."

"I have no doubt. Anyway, I'm sorry your brother's role in this came as such a shock to you."

"How did you meet him?"

I heard his face crack into a smile. "A rebel never tells another rebel's secrets. We met through others, that's as much as you need to know."

"I see. More secrets." Here, I implied that he never told me his name. To be honest, I grew tired of asking him. If he wanted to tell me, fine. If not, fine.

"Ah, this again."

"Never mind. I don't care anymore. But back to Colvin. I figured we all have to fight for something, I guess. He might as well fight for what's right instead of going along with what's wrong."

"For once, you sound like a reasonable person," he teased.

I ignored the remark and instead listened to the sound of our breathing fill the room. Part of me wanted to reach out and touch his chest, feel the rise and fall of his breaths.

"There was another reason I came to see you."

Because you wanted to kiss me? I couldn't help it, it was the first thought that came to me. There was no reason why that should be the single thought in my mind, but it was. Then I realized why...because those romantic feelings I held for him as a child never vanished. Over the years, the myth and mystery of this man had only grown, strengthening in my mind until he wasn't merely human any more — he was much, much more than that. To have this phantom of the rebels in my room, all alone, at night, made the workings of my brain whirl in the direction of seduction.

It really wasn't that far-fetched of a thought. He was handsome and intriguing and probably chased after by a thousand women every day. Yes, I thought sarcastically, sign me up for *that* list. Let me be number one thousand and one, nothing other than a thoughtless conquest in the dead of night.

No thank you.

"What's the other reason you're here, in my room, under cover of darkness and without my parents' permission?" I asked smartly.

He chuckled. Then one of his fingers found my cheek and traced it to my chin. "My intentions aren't surreptitious."

"No? Your actions are."

"Anna, it's very risky for me to go out during the day. In case you haven't noticed, I'm a wanted man."

His finger still rested on my chin. For a moment, I imagined what that hand would feel like on my breast. Oh, I'd had a boy's hand on my breast before. One boy's hands in particular had touched more than that, but he was dead now. A patriot loyalist killed in a skirmish outside Franklin.

The feel of someone else's hand and the pleasure it brought wasn't new to me, but neither was it fresh in my mind. And I wanted it to be fresh. I wanted it now, so I forced the thought into the back of my mind, where hopefully it would disappear.

"I know you're a wanted man. I'm well aware of that."

His finger trickled down my neck.

He sighed. "While you're in the city, you have to keep your visits outside to a minimum."

"What?" I almost shouted.

The finger covered my lips. The bed groaned as he leaned forward. He smelled of spiced soap. That was a luxury, to be sure. I was used to castile soap, and unless you had herbs to perfume it, it smelled like very little. Branthe, on the other hand, smelled of cloves and lavender. It made me jealous to inhale it on him.

"For your own safety, you have to stay indoors. Until the reds stop looking for you and you're able to move away with your family, those are the rules."

"But I don't understand. There aren't any more cameras, so there are no pictures of me. A red who didn't know me couldn't recognize me."

He touched the top of my head as if I was a child he was saying goodnight to. "They can recognize you. Though ordinary citizens only have papers, the government still uses pictures. They have the technology, they just won't give it to us. Believe me when I tell you they know exactly what you look like. Any of the officers in town could recognize you in an instant and you'd be back in the arms of Mann."

A metallic taste filled my mouth. "Well, I don't want that."

"Me neither," he mumbled.

There was something in the way he said it that made my ears perk up. Taking a risk, I reached out and touched him under the throat. His shirt was open and the skin smooth, beckoning to be felt. I was a more than willing participant. His heartbeat pulsed beneath my fingers and the intimacy of the moment woke my body.

Though I wanted to run my hand down to feel the lines of his chest and abdomen, I stopped myself. I felt that if I went any farther, he would stop me. But I could've been wrong. It wouldn't be the first time.

He squeezed the hand that rested at his open collar. "Stay safe. If you must go out, make sure there are plenty of people about. That way, you'll be just another face in the crowd. It'll lessen your chance of being recognized."

As much as I didn't want to, I acquiesced. "Yes, sir."

The bed creaked as he rose and in one, two, three steps, he crossed the room and escaped out the window before I had a chance to say goodbye.

CHAPTER TEN

"If you promise to do exactly as I say, I'll take you outside," Colvin said several mornings later.

Crossing my heart, I replied, "I promise to do exactly as you say."

His eyebrows rose in disbelief but his words were true enough. "All right. First things first. You must stick to me like glue. No matter what."

I nodded.

"Secondly, don't look any of the reds in the eye."

This was new to me. "Why not?"

He pulled a pack of smuggled cigarettes from his pocket and proceeded to strike a match against the rough stone of the fireplace.

"Those aren't good for you, you know."

He held the burning stick to the end of the tobacco-filled treat. "Anna, I only get them once a month, if that. I think I'll be okay."

"Suit yourself. But if you get cancer the government isn't going to do anything about it."

With a quick pucker of his lips, he blew out the match and tossed it into the fireplace. "That's the least of my problems. Anyway, as I was saying, or *not* saying since you decided to talk about my personal habits...we believe, but can't verify for certain, that the reds have some sort of face recognition technology. It looks like a very small eyeglass that's only worn over one eye. Have no doubt that they possess a picture of you and that if you make eye contact with one of their soldiers, your face will be screened against a database of thousands. Don't make eye contact."

My mind whirled to a man in red with a contraption made of iron and glass discreetly placed over his eye like a monocle. As he looked from face to face, a computer behind the glass scrolled through thousands of faces and names, trying to match each to a rebel or rogue.

I positioned the cloak over my shoulders and pulled the hood well up over my head. "Well then, are you ready to go?"

"Where is it you wanted to go again?"

"Anywhere," I replied, exhausted of being stuck in the small house with only my parents as company, for Branthe hadn't returned since that first night and probably never would.

"There's an old church near here. It's mostly ruins now but the stained glass is something to see."

"Won't they think it odd we're going there?"

He shook his head and dashed the cigarette against the hearth. "Not at all. Lots of people go there, though they're mostly beggars."

"Beggars?" The alarm in my voice must've amused him for Colvin smiled.

"Don't worry. Where I'm taking you, none of the beggars ever go there."

"Why's that?"

He smiled secretly. "You'll see."

Great. Just what I wanted. A surprise in the midst of all this. "All right. Let's go. What are we waiting for?" I asked impatiently.

He pulled on his own cloak and replied, "Nothing at all. Absolutely nothing."

CHAPTER ELEVEN

It was easy enough to keep the cloak pulled up over my head and my face down. That was no problem. The hard part was keeping my expression stoic as I witnessed, for the first time, what life in a city had become.

A large line of people, at least two blocks long, formed outside a storefront. The building was nondescript, a simple black face with large-paned windows. We were in the old part of the city, where the buildings were smaller and dingy compared to the new city, where everything was tall and made of marble. I hadn't seen that part, only heard about it from Colvin.

"What are they lining up for?" I asked, turning toward him just enough to make eye contact.

He leaned close to me. "Their daily food ration. A few of them might have room in their yard for a garden, but most of them either don't want to plant one or didn't grow enough food to keep them."

"How does it work?"

He pushed a strand of blond hair back from his forehead. "You show papers proving how many are in your household and you wait. Sometimes you get one loaf of bread, sometimes they throw in a block of cheese. Sometimes it's only flour. It depends."

"So everyone's accounted for," I mumbled.

"Now you get it," he smirked.

We walked in silence through the crowd, weaving past the steady stream of people. Having only taken washcloth baths for the past week since there wasn't much water to go around, I felt grubby compared to what life had been like. But as my eyes drifted over the crowd, I quickly realized even that was a luxury. Most of these people were dirty, and it wasn't just a smudge of dirt on a cheek. It was dirt-matted hair, neck-folds full of grease, and soot around the corners of their eyes.

They looked to be merely existing. If I didn't hate the reds before, now I despised them. No one lived to the fullest. This wasn't freedom. It was being chained to a system that kept you dependent on them for food, shelter, everything you needed. It was grotesque.

The crimson coat of a guard caught my attention. He stood in the doorway of a building, scanning the crowd. He didn't face me and I wanted to see if one of those monocles was rooted in his eye. I willed him to look my way.

My heart sped up. Colvin's warning about not being seen drummed in my head. I just needed him to look a little more to the right, but not at me. *Look a little more to the right.*

An older man wearing a crumpled tricorn hat approached us, swaggering left and right. My glance shifted from the guard to the man and back. His unfocused eyes stared at me. No, past me. I looked away, trying to avoid his glance, but he continued walking toward us. As I made to pass him in the street, his hands shot out. He yelled something incomprehensible, clutched my cloak and fell to the ground.

The guard I'd been eyeing saw everything. He pushed against the wave of people, coming straight for us. With his focus on the man, it was my one chance to see if he wore the stupid monocle that diverted my attention in the first place...he wasn't. Not a bit of glass or iron to be seen anywhere on his face.

Hands unhooked the man from my cloak. A crowd had gathered, pawing at him. They probably wanted his loose change. Alive and breathing, albeit moaning, he thrashed about aimlessly.

"Let's go," Colvin said, grabbing my arm.

"But he needs help," I argued.

"Are you a doctor? You can't help him." He tugged me through the throng of people.

Within minutes the whole thing became a distant memory as we wound through the cobble streets. If I'd been forced to find the way back on my own, I never would've made it. Just when I thought we could go no deeper in the city, I saw the church.

Two great spires jutted into the heavens like fingers forever trying to touch God. Between them, clad in gray stone, lay a rose window constructed of fuchsias, blues, golds, greens and whites. Though broken in a few places, most likely by vandals throwing rocks, the majority of the window remained perfectly intact. For a moment, I stood and gaped. It was beyond beautiful. It held an indescribable majesty.

"Want to go in?" Colvin asked, smiling.

"Yes," I said breathlessly.

The inside held rubbish and scattered pews. A dark spot sat in one corner. It was the fire pit, probably used by the beggars he'd told me about. Speaking of which...

"Where are the beggars?"

"Oh they're not here during the day."

"So you were just trying to scare me."

"What else are big brothers for?"

I elbowed him.

"Come. There's more."

"More?" I muttered. It was hard to believe there could be any more. But in the back of the church one of the walls had crumbled. Beyond the gaping hole stood a view of the city that proved unparalleled. From the hillside, Corinth looked like a quaint town from days of old. Smoke rose from houses, billowing into the sky like puffs of ebony cotton balls. A few mechanical wagons blustered down the brick roads of Old Town, sputtering as they rolled down the way. From here, it looked peaceful, almost like a place one would want to live. I got dreamy-eyed just watching it.

"What are you doing here?" a voice snarled behind us.

We both whirled. The redcoat was young, but built like a bull. He sneered at us, as if hoping to find two people he could arrest for loitering.

Colvin, of course, flashed a charming smile. That was my brother for you, never ruffled by anything.

"I was showing her the view," he said.

The man scowled. It was then I noticed it. The glass monocle in his right eye. I gave Colvin a wide-eyed look. He replied with a nod so slight, if I hadn't been looking for it I would've missed it.

"You've shown her, so move on. This is restricted territory."

"Of course," my brother replied.

My heartbeat drummed in my ears. The soldier stood by the door, obviously waiting for us to leave, which meant we had to pass right in front of him. My cowl was still pulled low, so he couldn't see my face as I crossed the sanctuary.

Colvin walked beside me, keeping his body between me and the red. We neared the door with only a few footfalls left when the soldier's hand grabbed my cloak.

"Let me see your face."

I froze, my body unable to work. My mouth wouldn't move to form an excuse nor did my legs pump to run.

"My sister isn't well, sir. She's been sick and is still getting over it. We did everything we could to make sure the rest of us didn't catch it, but it left her scarred. The pockmarks haven't all healed. I don't think she's contagious anymore but you never know."

His grand speech stopped the red for half a second, at most. He then replied with a smirk and repeated his command for me to lower my cowl. At this point, I felt there was no other choice, so I did as he said.

A tiny red light on the side of the monocle flashed and then he pulled his pistol. His hand shook as if this was the first time he'd ever arrested anyone. Not the confident red I expected.

"You're coming with me, both of you. Anna Hinton, you're under arrest on the charge that you're an escaped criminal."

"Of course," Colvin said. But instead, he grabbed the pistol and yanked it from the man. The soldier was so surprised he looked down at his fingers as if waiting for the gun to jump back into his hand.

"Give me the eyepiece." Colvin's voice was steady. Gone was my lackadaisical older brother and in his place stood a rebel.

The man did as he was told.

"Does this connect immediately and send the information or do you have to hook it into a port?"

The red shook his head, confused. "I charge it every night. That's all."

"Do they know you've seen us?" Colvin's voice tightened.

"I don't know."

His voice rose. "I'll ask only once more and then I'll shoot your left eye out." He spoke with slow deliberation. "Do *they* know you've seen her?"

"I don't know," he yelled, his voice wavering. "I don't think so." He thought about it for a moment. "No, they don't. I have to report it. I only receive the pictures, it doesn't transmit that I've made a match."

He exhaled in relief and for a brief second, looked down. The red made his move, lurching for the gun. Colvin moved by instinct, chambering and then firing the bullet that ultimately lodged in the center of the man's chest.

I tried to scream. I wanted to scream, but nothing came out. In the end, I watched as the man slumped to the floor, gurgling and coughing blood until he bled out. When he stilled, I checked for a pulse, just to make sure there wasn't one.

"He's dead."

Without a word, Colvin took my hand and led me out through the rear of the church. We slid down the hillside, thorns and dirt matting my dress and hair. When we reached the bottom, we broke into a run, not stopping until we reached the center of Old Town and the hustle and bustle of the doomed city. We didn't cease our walk until we made it to the house, where Colvin deposited me with my parents. I spent the next hour on my bed, crying, wishing for once in my life that I could take a hot bath and forget any of this existed.

CHAPTER TWELVE

This time, I heard the quiet jiggle of the window as it was unlocked, from the outside I might add, and opened.

"You've come to chastise me," I said before he had a chance to speak.

I heard his foot touch the rug. He paused and then shut the window behind him. "What makes you say that?"

"Why else would you be here? I'm sure Colvin told you what happened and now you're here to tell me that I shouldn't have pressured my brother into letting me go outside."

The bed sagged as he sat down. "Well, you shouldn't have."

"A man was killed today." The words flew out of my mouth with sadness I didn't expect.

"I know. Even if your brother hadn't told me, I would've known anyway."

"How?"

"The reds are going door to door, checking that everyone is who they say. Your parents have new papers and their images aren't registered with the Patriot Party. You, on the other hand, your image is registered. So, we have a couple of choices."

I knew I wasn't going to like this. "They are?"

"You can stay here. When the house is searched tomorrow, you can hide under the floorboards in the living room. I've already shown your father where they are."

"And the other choice?"

"You can leave with me now. I'll slip you through a few barricades and then you can be placed back at the house you were in a few days ago until the manhunt dies down."

"Leave my family again? No thanks. I'll hide here."

"All right. As there's no telling when they'll come and I won't be able to be here, you'll need to be placed there at first light."

"To stay all day?"

"Yes."

My response was a tart, "Fine. Now that you've said your piece, you can leave." My own anger at him surprised me. Dear Lord, for my entire life I'd fantasized about him, wanting to touch his hair and face, talk to him, know about the mysterious Branthe, and now I was being a grade-A bitch. But the truth was he hadn't come to see if I was okay, he was only coming to tell me how my life was once again going to get worse before it got better.

He replied with a soft sigh. "Such irreverence, Anna. Really, for a man who saved you from the clutches of Colonel Mann, I thought I deserved a little more thanks than that. Especially since I brought something for you."

"Thank you for saving me then and for warning me now. I suppose you think I owe you something."

He paused. When he spoke, his voice was so sad it made my heart want to break. "No, I don't think you owe me anything nor would I want you to feel that way."

"But I do owe you."

The darkness in the bedroom had lightened, my eyes adjusting to the face and body in front of me. His white shirt sat open at the throat, once more willing me to touch his skin. I ignored the temptation and focused instead on his soulful eyes.

"Tell me what happened when you were little," he requested.

"You mean when you saved us?"

"If that's what you want to call it, yes."

So I did, trying my best to make him sound dark and heroic and me not quite so young and fragile, as if that would jog his memory of the event.

"And my father turned to thank you, but you were gone."

"I slinked away like a coward."

I swatted his hand. "How dare you say that! I prefer to think you moved on to save someone else."

"Is that what you think of me? That I'm so courageous I'm out prowling every night, looking for defenseless people to save?"

"Would it be silly of me to think so?"

With my hand still resting on his, he tilted his palm toward mine and enclosed it. "No, it wouldn't be silly at all if I was that man. But I'm not. I hide in the shadows, fighting my enemy in the dark, waiting for the right opportunity."

"You think so little of yourself. It makes me sad."

He placed his other hand atop mine. "Well, we don't want you to be sad. I didn't come here for that. Tell me something instead that makes you happy."

I laughed. His fingers pressed against my lips like a stopper. "We don't want to wake your parents."

I nodded and he released his fingers only to rest them once again on my hand. Thinking for a moment, I decided to tell him about life with my family in the country and about how silly Colvin was growing up. Within minutes, I had him laughing. Even in the near darkness, I saw tears in the corner of his eyes. I smiled as he worked diligently to contain his amusement so that we wouldn't wake my parents.

"So he really tried to burn the barn down?"

"He did. He was a little pyromaniac."

"And your father found him?"

"Found him looking for matches and gave him the worst tan hiding I'd ever seen."

He wiped away a tear. "I'll have to mention that next time I see him. And what about you? What were you like?"

"Me?" I shrugged. "Just as boring as I am now."

"The last thing you are is boring."

I became acutely aware of the hand holding mine and how, with great tenderness, his thumb gently stroked my palm. I met his eyes and we sat there, staring at one another. I wanted him to kiss me. I felt it desperately, as if my soul wanted to reach out and get entangled in his soul. Never in my life had these feelings arose in me. I not only wanted Branthe, I needed him and every molecule in my body seemed to agree.

"You said you brought something for me?"

"Yes." He placed something in my palm. It was rectangular with paper wrapping. It took half a second before I realized what it was.

"Chocolate! Where did you get it?"

"If I tell you that, I'll have to kill you."

I giggled. It couldn't be helped. Chocolate was so scarce no common person ever saw it. Then I thought about it. Rumors abounded that the only people who were able to get it were government officials, which he clearly wasn't.

I handed it back to him. "Who *did* you kill to get this?"

"I didn't kill anyone. There was a raid on a supply wagon last night. Among other things, my men recovered this. You're welcome, by the way."

"Thank you," I mumbled.

I felt his fingers on my hair. I swear he was half-cat, as he could see way better at night than I could ever dream. I saw the white of his shirt as well as the whites of his eyes, but beyond that, he sat drenched in darkness.

"Do you want to stay?" I asked, shocked at my own directness.

He sighed. "Anna, do you know what it is to be with me?"

"No, of course not." *That's the point of you staying,* I wanted to add.

His fingers cascaded down my cheek, coming to rest on my chin and then my throat. Hadn't we done this before?

"I wouldn't wish my life on you. There's no glamour in it. It's all hiding. Who I am can't be revealed, not to anyone."

"I'm already a fugitive. So are you. What does any of the rest of it matter?"

"It matters to me."

Then I did it. I couldn't help it. Being so close to him, to this man I'd wanted for so long, dreamt of for so long, I let boldness and brazenness overcome me. I lifted his hand and placed it on my breast. My nightgown was thin, a *shift*, the term we were all supposed to use for it. The thin muslin, practically transparent in daylight, now puckered from my raised nipple. I swirled his thumb against it, wanting him to feel it tighten under his touch.

I thought he'd pull away, but he didn't. His thumb remained, moving on its own. My breath became shallow as I waited to see what he'd do next. He continued swirling his finger, making the nipple as hard as it could get. Then he clasped his mouth over it.

I managed not to yell out in surprise, but couldn't contain a small gasp. It was enough of a disturbance that he lifted his head. Feeling in the dark, I placed a hand on either side of his face and brought his lips to mine.

It wasn't the kiss of an inexperienced adolescent trying to figure out what to do. Branthe parted his lips, letting his tongue slowly slip over mine. The fragrance of cloves flashed over my taste buds. He was delicious.

My tongue met his, entwining with it. He caressed my lips with short kisses, each time his tongue probing me. I willingly reciprocated, feeling the heat rise in my body with each kiss. My nipples were hard now, wanting to be stroked, needing to be touched. I picked up his hand and placed it back on my breast.

This time, he squeezed the nipple, bringing me to the point of pain. I felt beneath his waistcoat and shirt to the smooth skin of his chest. I found his own nipple, twisting it until he pushed me back on the bed. My fingers worked quickly, unbuttoning his waistcoat and tearing off his shirt.

When I reached his breeches, I rubbed the bulge. He was as ready as I was. More so, it seemed. His hands tightened at the bottom of my shift and I felt it rise over my hips. Sitting up, I allowed him to raise the thin cloth over my head. He kissed every inch of my body as it was uncovered. When the only thing I wore was my skin, Branthe gently pushed me onto my back.

He ran his tongue down my neck to my breasts. He sucked and pulled, nibbled and rolled each peak between his teeth until I was about to cry out his name. Reaching for the buttons of his breeches, I found they were beyond my fingers. I rolled my eyes, knowing this was exactly what he wanted.

His fingers danced their way down my skin to the warm spot between my legs. He stroked my damp hair, flicking his fingers gently up and down the spot of pleasure. Rolling to one side, he suckled my nipple as his fingers worked their way inside me. Without a word, he edged down between my legs.

He raised each leg, bending it at the knee and then parting them. Kneeling at my opening, I waited for him to unbutton his breeches. God, how I wanted him to. But instead, I felt the warmth of his tongue as it worked me, licking my juice away and jutting into me. He toyed with me, letting his tongue swirl all around. Then Branthe pushed his fingers inside. He stroked me, his fingers working in and out while his tongue nibbled at my small mound of flesh until a shudder shifted my body from pure pleasure to release.

I lay on the bed, body exposed but I didn't care. After a moment, he came to me. He cupped my face in his hands and kissed me. Spent and ready for nothing but sleep, still I ran my hands down his chest to his groin. A low moan pushed through his lips. Then he took my wrist and brought it up to his face.

"I don't want that from you, not tonight."

Oh. So then what just happened?

"What do you want? To give me pleasure and be done with it? To give in to me just enough that you won't have to do any more than that?"

He sighed. "As I said, being with me isn't easy. I wouldn't wish it on any woman, most of all you."

"Why not?"

Without a word, he dressed and crept back to the window. "Some things are better left sacred. Women are paired and married based on sexual history. Surely you know that."

"Of course. The Rendering."

"Once you're cleared of any charges and allowed to return to society, you'll be married based on that. Keep your virginity and you'll marry better."

"How will my name ever be cleared now? I'm a rebel, remember? Same as you."

"Don't worry. I have my ways, Anna. I'm doing this for you." With that, he escaped the conversation out the window.

Doing this for me. I snuggled under the covers. For all the pleasure he'd just given me, Branthe left me feeling hopeless. If he was doing this for me, why did I feel so used, so wanton and so inexplicably void of emotion?

He didn't wish himself on any woman, *most of all me.* He was leaving me intact (so he thought) because he didn't want to ruin me. Well, he already had. I was ruined from the first moment I saw him.

CHAPTER THIRTEEN

The next day, the house was searched just as he said it would be. My hiding spot under the floorboards, though dank and cold, served its purpose — I wasn't found. Branthe didn't come to check on me that night, nor the next. I wasn't surprised. He'd probably never enter my window again, afraid I'd seduce him into doing something that would destroy the rest of my life.

After all, he'd all but told me we couldn't be together. No matter how much I wanted it, we never would be, so there was no point in holding out any hope.

The news devastated me. Yes, devastated. That's exactly how I felt, but I did my best not to let it show. Colvin and my parents, if they noticed, said nothing. They probably thought it just the drudgery of the city getting to me, which was also true. The more I lived there, the more I noticed how grimy and filthy the place and the people were.

More than that, I started noticing the rounding up of young women. Though very subtle, it went the same way every time — two soldiers appeared at the door of the home. The door opened and they entered. When they left, they escorted a young woman between them. After a few hours, she always returned alone. The look on each girl's face appeared the same — eyes drawn together and mouth frowning, as if something had been taken from her.

It took some time, but I finally stumbled into a regular routine of knitting, cooking, and reading, getting used to my small prison. This monotonous repetition, though comforting in some ways, made every day seem the same – long and boring. So when, on a rather nondescript day of performing the same mundane chores, a knock sounded at the front door, I was surprised.

The three of us sat in the living room. Pop read from a copy of *Tom Sawyer* that he'd procured from Colvin, while Mom and I worked by the fire. She mended socks while I fixed the hem on one of my dark muslin dresses.

As soon as the knock sounded, we glanced at one another, eyes shining with apprehension. Pop set the book down and walked to the door.

"Who is it?" he asked.

"It's me," came Branthe's reply. That he assumed my father knew the sound of his voice seemed either the height of arrogance or telling of the depth of their friendship. I didn't know which held the truth.

Pop's hand, resting with hesitation on the lock, quickly released the bolt and welcomed him inside. It had been nearly a month (not that I was counting) since my eyes had been given the pleasure of his beauty.

And beauty he encompassed. I'd almost forgotten how his eyes, framed with long lashes, gave him a haunted, yearning look. His straight nose and jawline possessed an aristocratic yet masculine flair that made me (and probably a thousand women) want to throw myself at him. Finally, his broad shoulders could rest a woman atop each one, both of whom would be fighting over him, of course.

"Is everything all right?" my father asked.

Branthe closed and bolted the door behind him. He surveyed the room, greeting us. "Mrs. Hinton, Miss Hinton, good evening."

"Good evening to you," my mother replied.

"Please, sit down," he said to my father, who did what he said, but with hesitation. Branthe took a deep inhale before starting. "Colvin, as you may or may not be aware, went on a raid two nights ago."

My father shook his head. "He doesn't tell us anything of this business. He says the less we know, the better."

"And that couldn't be more true. It's for your own protection. The less you know, the less likely it is you can be harmed." As the last few words left his lips, his eyes cascaded to me. My face immediately flushed with heat. Though no one watched, my face, throat and ears burned under his gaze. Good thing the candlelight didn't illuminate the room very well.

"Colvin's gone on raids before. That's nothing new, but this time the reds must've been tipped off. They were waiting for us."

My head started pounding. I looked at my father and mother. The blood emptied from both their faces. They, as well as I, were expecting the worst.

"Is he...Is he dead?" Pop asked.

"No," came the quick reply. Branthe pulled a wooden chair from a corner and centered it as close to us as the coffee table in the middle of the room allowed. "He's been captured. By Colonel Mann."

My throat dried and if my heart could've stopped beating, it would have. I feared for my brother's safety under the watch of the colonel. If he discovered Colvin's relationship to me, it would be mean torture, if not death for him.

"So he's at the prison," Pop said.

"For now, but I've received word that he's to be moved."

"Is this person to be trusted?"

Branthe nodded. "I would trust him with my life. The good news is that, unless Mann's plans change, they'll be traveling through Corinth."

"When?" I blurted.

His eyes flickered to mine, his gaze cool and detached. "I don't have word on the exact day, but I should know soon."

"I can help you," I said, chiming in again.

"Anna," Pop said, shushing me.

"I can. I know what the colonel looks like. Do any of your men know what he looks like?"

Branthe smiled at me with pity. "I believe the entourage will be large enough for us to gather exactly which one the colonel is. We shouldn't need your help in this. Besides, if Mann saw you, your life would be forfeit."

I wouldn't be deterred. "But neither you nor your other man saw him when you rescued me. Do you know what he looks like?"

"As I said - from his entourage, we'll know him."

"So you don't," I replied triumphantly.

His cool gaze hardened. He opened his mouth to make some regal retort but my mother beat him to it.

"Anna, you'd do best to stay out of their way. Your place is here."

Seeing that this wasn't an argument I would win, I nodded.

"Mr. Hinton, I may need your help in some things, if that's all right with you. We must be ready when Mann arrives. We'll have to work with stealth and speed if we hope to free Colvin."

Pop clasped his hands together. "Anything. Ask anything of us and we'll be happy to oblige."

Branthe stood. "Thank you. Perhaps it would be best if we discussed this further in your study."

Father pawed at the pocket of his quilted waistcoat. He searched for tobacco, a treat he smoked in a pipe only at night. My mother abhorred his guilty pleasure, rolling her eyes every time he partook, but she said nothing. Life was too hard to nitpick about small things. He kissed my mother and me on the forehead and then led Branthe into the next room, lighting his pipe on the way out.

***

"You need to stay out of this," Branthe said later, having arrived in my room only moments before.

He took his usual place on my bed, but sat closer to the end than usual.

"I didn't realize that I'm contagious," I said smartly.

"Don't start, Anna. What happened the last time I was here is neither here nor there. I'm talking about Colvin."

I disagreed completely. "Then why do I feel used? As If you got from me what you wanted and that's all I'm worth."

He sighed heavily. "Would it change things if I declared my undying love for you?"

I laughed quietly. "Go ahead," I replied, knowing he wouldn't.

He paused long enough for me to wonder if he would actually do it. "There was once a girl I cared for very much, almost as much as...well I cared for her, let's say that. We were very close and I was about to ask for her hand when she disappeared."

"This was before the war?"

He nodded. "Right after it started. Anyway, she simply vanished. No one claimed to know where she was. I asked her parents - they didn't know anything. I asked her siblings, cousins, uncles, aunts - anyone and everyone, but all swore they knew nothing about where she'd gone. Then one night I received a letter from her. Technology had disappeared by this time, so the letter came by mail. I immediately went to her and discovered that one of our friends had gotten her pregnant and insisted she abort the child. The termination occurred late in the first trimester and the doctor was nothing less than an unfeeling butcher. She died in my arms."

He paused, giving me ample time to say something, but nothing came. Nothing witty or charming or even sympathetic flew into my mind.

"You loved her?"

"Very much. It broke my heart. Not so much that she ran off with another man, but what he did to her. I'm sure you're wondering why I burdened you with this." He took my hand. "Anna, I can't go through that again, not with anyone, no matter how much I care about them."

So here sat Branthe, wanton and rogue, admitting he felt something for me. I thought when this moment came (if it ever did) that elation would overtake me. I thought I'd jump up and down on my bed, screaming from excitement. But mainly, I thought the news would make me happy.

Instead, it made me angry. "So you deny yourself and someone else, mainly *me*, happiness? And you're doing it because you might get hurt? Is that right?"

"Not only me. You might as well."

"Have you seen the world you live in? Do you see the misery that's out there? This - you and me, could hold happiness. It would be the one shining star in an otherwise meager existence. It would be worth something. It would make this life worth *something*."

"Anna—"

"Don't. Don't tell me I'm being foolish or childish because I'm not. What do we have if not each other? The world is upside down and you're about the only thing in my life that's right side up. Do you feel the same?"

"It doesn't matter how I feel."

His words sucked the air from me. I leaned back against the bedframe and replied, "Then I can't help you and I don't want to. If you think your feelings are inconsequential, then I'm happy to say goodnight and wish you well."

He didn't wait for me to change my mind. Branthe escaped out the window in a flash. Good. Saying his feelings about me didn't matter was akin to hearing I didn't matter. With that thought churning in my mind, I decided I never wanted to see Branthe again.

CHAPTER FOURTEEN

The next morning, my objective became freeing Colvin. While my father worked in another room, I snuck into his study, hoping to discover what happened in there the night before.

The most beautiful room in the house, the study radiated opulence. The past owner obviously cared very much for it, for the furnishings were wood or velvet and there was nothing cheap about either. My father liked the room too, for the cherry desk facing the door boasted a fresh coat of oil. Its sheen reflected the sunlight and made the room brighter. A creeping vine carved into the legs and overhanging lip looked as if it had been chiseled from the wood only yesterday, so perfect were the angles and lines.

Of course, nothing on the desk betrayed what the two had done. I looked around the room, peering in the built-in bookcases, searching for anything that seemed out of order. My eyes drifted until I came to the hearth. Cold black coals sat atop the grate. It hadn't been lit yesterday, I knew that for certain. I gave it a cursory glance before moving on.

Wait.

Something the color of dark cream sat atop the coals. I looked closer.

"Yes, I think I've got one of those. Let me check my study."

Pop's voice drifted in from the kitchen. Without thinking, I snatched the paper, stuffed it down my dress and threw open the door, coming face to face with my father.

"Oh, there you are!" I said, in what hoped to be a good cover. "I was looking for you."

"You could've knocked to find out if I was in my study or not," he said, obviously annoyed.

"I know, but sometimes you fall asleep with your head on the desk."

He searched my face. Looking for a lie, I knew. But I kept my features expressionless, or else he'd suspect something.

"You've found me. What do you want?"

"I need to know if you want carrots or potatoes with dinner?"

"Potatoes, I think."

"Good. Me too."

With that, I sidestepped him and fled to my room. I locked the door behind me and pulled the sheet of paper from my breast. It left a mess of ash on my skin, which I brushed away. When I opened it, I noted that most of the words were gone save for a few.

Lord Andrews...masque on the eve of October 31...Colonel Mann...

I didn't recognize the handwriting but the message implied Mann planned to attend this masque. Lord Andrews… Where did I know that name? It hit me. Colonel Mann's desk held a letter from Lord Andrews. In it, the letter stated this lord lived in Corinth. So that meant Andrews would host the masque? Yes, I was sure of it. The rebels knew all of this, but how would they get in? They didn't have ties to the new aristocracy. At least, none that I knew of.

I burned what remained of the message in the waste bin in the corner of my room. That bastard had my brother. If I couldn't help the rebels free him, I would at least extract my own revenge on him for everything he tried to do to me. I knew that where he failed with me, there had to be women who hadn't been so lucky to escape. I was doing this for them, too.

Was my anger in part created by the conversation with Branthe the night before? More than likely, but I didn't care. Tired of being an object to one man and less than nothing to another, I set out to prove my worth.

I had to be there the night of the masque, even if it meant risking my own freedom. As far as I knew, there was only one way to do this.

I had to get a job at Lord Andrews' mansion.

CHAPTER FIFTEEN

I snuck out the next morning. Knowing my parents would worry, and rightly so, I left them a short but cryptic note regarding my whereabouts. After asking a few people on the street, I quickly found myself headed in the direction of Andrews' mansion.

Guards didn't watch the alleys, so that's the way I traveled. Definitely not the cleanest path, as people threw trash out their back windows, but it was the most secure way to go. Though I risked arriving with a skirt full of feces, I also ensured my safety. Feces could be cleaned off, I reasoned with myself. Prison and possible hanging couldn't.

The mansion sat on a hill in Old Town. It was the better part of Old Town, with dress shops and merchants lining the roads. The area was clean of debris and smelled much nicer than the part I was from. A wrought-iron gate protected the front of the white colonial mansion, making the place look impenetrable. On closer inspection, I noticed a cobblestone road running toward the rear. Experience taught me that if I wanted a job, I needed to go to the back door, not the front, where I would be laughed at by the butler.

As I trekked my way up the back path, the thunder of hoofs sounded ahead. Rolling down the hill toward me at breakneck speed roared a black carriage drawn by four horses. I threw myself onto an ivy wall, barely escaping the carriage's path before the driver barreled down on me.

"Get out of the way!" he yelled.

Don't worry, I have no intention of dying today.

Once the carriage passed, presumably carrying the master of the house, I made my way to the back door and knocked. An older woman with globs of dough on her hair answered the door.

"Well, what is it?" she asked impatiently.

"I'm looking for work."

She eyed me up and down. Her short, gray hair framed her face like a bunch of frayed wires. For a moment it felt like she saw into my soul. Sweat sprinkled my forehead.

Finally, she said, "Well come in, we could use some help."

CHAPTER SIXTEEN

Though the mansion appeared huge on the outside, I deemed it manageable based on my experience at the colonel's. Mrs. Peele, for that was the name of the woman who hired me, put me to work in the kitchen, which wasn't exactly what I had in mind, but it would do. Working in the kitchen meant I didn't have access to the rest of the house the way someone of the upstairs staff would. That limited my knowledge of the place and its residents, though I was told Lord Andrews was the only occupant.

A bachelor, he never married, though there were plenty of eligible women in town and plenty who wouldn't mind marrying him, Mrs. Peele assured me, for he was handsome.

Even working down below I still heard gossip, particularly about the masque. Invitations posted a few weeks earlier to the upper-crust of Corinth and neighboring towns. I confirmed the date as Halloween, making the letter I snatched from Pop's study correct. I was, of course, expected to work that night, which I agreed to happily.

My parents, on the other hand, weren't happy. However, I gave them much of my earnings and promised to stay out of the reds' sight, which remained easy since I moved through alleys to and from work. I had settled into a comfortable routine when Mrs. Peele came to me one evening after the dinner service.

"Peggy doesn't feel well. If you ask me, that girl's gone and got herself in trouble." Meaning - pregnant. Pregnancy outside of marriage held the steep punishment of being ostracized from family and even the town. Mrs. Peele gave me the sort of look that said *don't you be doing anything foolish like that* and finished with, "Anyway, she's gone home. I need you to fetch the lord's tray from his study."

I barely knew the mansion, but I knew from her directions where to find the study. "Of course."

It was not lost on me that the last time I entered a private room it ended in disaster. But with chin up, I wiped my soapy hands on a towel and made my way up the back stairs to the main floor of the house. Candles were lit everywhere. Wall sconces, desk candelabras — if a flame could be lit on top of wax, it was. The place shone like no home I'd ever seen. Lord Andrews definitely lived on the plush side of wealthy.

With floorboards creaking and groaning beneath me, I walked down the hall to the third room on the left, the study. The door stood open. A fire burned in the hearth on the far wall and the built-in shelves were lined with tens if not hundreds of books. A desk sat empty on one side and in front of the hearth rested two leather chairs, the type men liked to smoke in after a meal.

Spying the tray on a side buffet by the wall across from the desk, I tiptoed over to it. I don't know why I tiptoed, there wasn't anyone in the room. The place just seemed too damned holy, as if any sound would break the spell of peace hovering over it. Shaking off my nerves, I picked up the tray and pivoted on my heel to walk back toward the door.

"You'll want to take this with you."

The tray slipped from one hand. I scrambled to hold onto it before it crashed to the floor. Silverware rattled atop the empty plates and I knew I was making a big fool out of myself. With the silver tray finally steady, I made my way to the hand holding the cup. Sitting in one of the chairs before the fire with his back to me, all I could see of the master of the house was a masculine arm and an outstretched hand delicately holding a china cup.

"What's your name?" he asked in a voice both deep and gruff. The timbre didn't match his physique. Though tempted to peer around the chair to see the face attached to the voice, I instead held my ground.

"My name's Anna," I replied.

"Anna, you'll want to be careful with the china in this house. It's more than five hundred years old and managed to survive the rebellion. I'd hate for a serving girl to be the reason why I lost even a single piece."

Humbled, my only reply was, "Yes, I'll be more careful." Then I took the cup and without a reasonable explanation as to why, I fled the room, glad to be gone from Lord Andrews' presence.

CHAPTER SEVENTEEN

Two weeks in, I'd collected enough wages to purchase what I needed — fabric. I scoured every bolt at one of the local shops to find a suitable pattern, but all the shopkeeper had were reams of dark muslin. After an hour or so, at the bottom of a bin of scraps, I discovered a bolt of silk. The color of a bluebird and embossed with gold thread, it was gorgeous.

The man kept his mouth shut when I said I wanted to purchase it, but I could tell his wheels were turning, trying to figure out how a girl like me could afford such extravagant fabric. Still, he let me purchase it and retained his opinions for himself. As soon as I got it home and every night thereafter, I set about turning it into what it needed to become.

I'd also managed to procure a few rhinestones and feathers from the shop. The mask was harder to make than I originally anticipated. Since glue's value had skyrocketed, making it expensive for a common person to procure, I did the next best thing — I made it from fabric, sewing all the decorations onto the facing.

UNLIKELY REBEL

As the night of the masque approached, the entire household buzzed. The kitchen stayed busy plucking chickens and pulling down pegs of smoked meat from the stores. Rumors abounded that we were expecting a special guest that evening, one who would stay the night. Apparently, the colonel's itinerary took him through Corinth on the way to Hashton Prison, where I assumed he needed to deposit Colvin. Why Mann escorted my brother himself was simply a question I couldn't answer. Having already learned it best not to ask too many questions, I kept mine silent and simply waited.

The day finally arrived. I stored the finished dress in my knapsack and took it to the kitchen with me, being sure to stash it under a little-used bench, where no one would find it. I still had no idea regarding how and what exactly I planned to do when I saw the colonel. My first hope was to see my brother alive. After that, I prayed a plan would fall into place.

Needless to say, I couldn't concentrate the entire day. My hands wouldn't knead dough correctly or whisk eggs fast enough. On more than one occasion, Mrs. Peele asked if I felt all right. I answered *yes* and made an attempt to focus harder on the job at hand.

Finally, near dusk, I heard the distinct rumble of Colonel Mann's mechanical carriage. I'd heard it what seemed a thousand times. It groaned when coming to a full stop – a sound that couldn't be mistaken for anything else.

I wanted to rush to one of the back windows and peek, but I contained myself, managing instead to mosey over while mixing cake batter. Sure enough, I saw the pockmarked fatty exiting his carriage.

Bringing up the rear came a mechanical wagon. Atop it sat a cage. Through the bars I spotted Colvin. It took all of my restraint not to cry out. He looked thin, but not emaciated. He appeared okay from afar, but the only way to know was to speak with him. But how?

"Too bad he's a prisoner," Mrs. Peele said, sneaking up beside me.

I almost dropped the bowl I held. "What do you mean?" I asked.

She spooned her batter into a pan that had been buttered and floured. "Looks like he would've made someone a fine husband if he hadn't been a rebel."

I almost choked on the words that came out next. "If you're not a patriot, you're a traitor, and it looks to me like whoever he is, he made the wrong choice in life."

She nodded. "True enough. Still, traitors need to eat. The men will dine with the lord shortly. I'll need someone to take him some food. Do you think you could stomach it?"

Stomach it? I almost jumped up and down with joy. Doing my best to put on an outer show of disgust, I snorted. "I suppose. Just make sure whatever he gets, it's cold and full of scraps meant for the pigs."

She made sure of that, all right. The plate I took held cooked potato peels and beef fat. My heart broke at the sight of it. I felt better knowing this meal was probably worlds better than whatever Mann fed him. But after this night, that would be a distant memory to Colvin.

I hoped.

Making my way out the back door, no one needed to tell me I couldn't dillydally around Colvin. I had to deliver the food and leave. But I needed information. Important information. To put it exactly, I needed to know who held the key to his cage.

He didn't see me approach. Good. I didn't want him to give anything away. As I got closer, I realized my brother looked terrible. Dark shadows in the shape of half moons filled the space beneath each eye. There were cuts and scraps across his face and his knuckles were bloody and crusted over. And that was only the skin I could see. I didn't want to think about what lay beneath his clothes.

I approached the guard on duty. He inspected the plate, being sure to spit a good-sized wad of phlegm into it.

"That should help fill him up," I said.

"You should add to it, too."

"Already did," I lied. "Got a good one in there." After poking it a few times, the guard let me pass. I reached the cage a moment later. His eyes were closed, so I made sure to speak good and loud.

"Slop for the swine."

He didn't move. My only chance to talk to my brother and it was about to go wrong. I did the only thing I could think of — I threw some of the food on his face. That woke him up. In fact, he awoke cursing, ready to fight. I laughed. It was an honest reaction. He blinked at me.

"It's too bad rebels have to be fed. It'd be better if they starved you," I mocked, spooning more slop onto the bed of the cage.

Colvin looked at me bleary-eyed before catching on. "I suppose you think we deserve less than that."

"The only thing you deserve is to rot on the hangman's noose." I threw more slop on the floor. "But if it must be one way or the other, I'm glad you're locked up without the possibility of getting out."

"You'd have to see Colonel Mann about that."

Keeping my head down, I lifted my eyes to his. Colvin winked at me. *Colonel Mann!* That's who held the key. Of course he did. Him I knew how to work. I only hoped he wouldn't know who was working him. I threw the rest of the food down.

"Enjoy one of your last meals, rebel. I hope you choke on it."

I turned my back and walked away from my brother. The next time I saw him, I expected to be setting him free.

CHAPTER EIGHTEEN

After dinner, the guests started to arrive. I'd never seen Mrs. Peele shout so many orders at the same time.

"Put cream on those! You, slice the bread! Make sure each cherry tomato is ripe before you place it on a cucumber!"

She worked me with no end in sight. I needed to leave. I had to change into the gown I'd worked on for two weeks and sneak into that party.

About an hour into it, I finally saw my chance. A tray of roasted mushrooms with goat cheese sat on the buffet getting cold. None of the upstairs servants arrived to pick them up and Mrs. Peele hadn't noticed.

"Those mushrooms will be ruined," I said, nodding toward them.

"Heavens to Betsy! Why haven't they been picked up?"

I wiped floured hands on my apron. "I'll take them up the back and give them to someone. Don't worry. If you can spare me for a moment, that is?"

She nodded her red face. "Hurry back, you'll be missed."

"Of course," I said.

With everyone's back turned away from me, I aimed for the plate. I planned to grab my knapsack and tray, stash the dress in a little-used broom closet on the back stairs, deliver the mushrooms and then return to the closet to change clothes. By the time my dress and mask were on, no one would recognize me.

With all eyes on food preparation, I thrust my hand beneath the bench that held my costume. I felt only air and wood. No. Someone couldn't have taken my bag. Trying not to panic, I scanned the room, but didn't see it anywhere.

"I thought you were taking those mushrooms up," Mrs. Peele snapped.

I straightened. "I am. I just dropped something."

"See that you find it and get moving."

"Yes, ma'am," I mumbled.

It was gone - nowhere to be found. My hopes sank. I had no choice but to take the tray upstairs. Maybe I would find it once I returned. Or maybe someone took it. There was no way to ask without drawing attention and possible suspicion.

Picking up the tray, I couldn't help but feel defeated before the night even started. My only other hope was that the rebels found a way into the party. I snickered. They were rebels, wanted men. There was no way they could finagle into the upper-crust of society like this. No possible way.

UNLIKELY REBEL

Lost in my thoughts, I almost didn't notice the brown sack jutting out from underneath a stool by the door. My bag! Someone had only moved it. With a quick look back to make sure no one watched, I reached down and tucked it beneath my arm and hurried up the stairs.

CHAPTER NINETEEN

I delivered the tray and snuck into the closet, lighting the small candle I'd stashed there a few days ago. I pulled the silk dress from the bag. It was a little crumpled, but nothing a sprinkle of water couldn't fix. I managed to change clothes in the meager light though I cussed a few times. Once the bodice was tightened and my petticoats straightened, I added the pièce de résistance — the mask.

Made of peacock feathers and clear crystals, it shimmered in the candlelight. The blue in the eye of the feathers matched the color of the dress perfectly.

Holding up a small mirror, I admired my reflection. Behind this mask I could be anyone. No longer was I a criminal, wanted for information. I transformed into a lady, ready to take my place among the other guests.

Feeling bold and ready, I stepped from the closet, though a little more tentatively than my newfound confidence suggested. After a quick look into the hallway to make sure it was clear, I crept up the stairs to the third floor and entered the ballroom.

A string quartet played in one corner of the room, the music sweeping over the crowd of masks. For a moment, I thought it would be impossible to find Mann in this sea of camouflage. But instinct knew better than my conscious mind. After a steady glance around the room, noting masks made of turkey feathers, plaster, and even fur, I listened for the high-pitched, nasal voice I knew in my nightmares.

He stood in a corner talking to a woman. His pudgy fingers, against all propriety, dangled over the square neckline of her dress, teasing the flesh of her breasts. I sighed. Someone beat me to him. Unless they separated, his attention would be stuck on her all night and my plan, useless.

A tray of complimentary foldout fans sat atop a side table. Picking one up, I flicked it open and cooled myself while I thought how to proceed next. My attention shifted to the rest of the room. That's when I saw him. He wore a mask of black crow feathers, but nothing could hide those dangerous brown eyes of his. Nothing.

My breath hitched as Branthe nodded at me. How on earth could he recognize me under a frilly mask and in an expensive dress? The same way I recognized him — by sense. For a moment, the romantic notion that only two people who were really meant to be together would know each other from afar, in disguise, and in a crowded room. Silly, I know, but the yearning I always felt when around him returned, this time stronger than before.

Surprisingly enough, my feelings weren't even marred by his last visit to my room.

He cut a path to me and I held my breath, hoping he'd walk right past me. His presence was a distraction. A nice one, but still a distraction.

He stopped and handed me a crystal cup of rum punch. "Care to join me in a drink?"

"Thank you," I murmured, embarrassed that he caught me trying to go behind the rebels' backs. Taking a small sip, I let the alcohol burn my mouth before swallowing. It was good. I wouldn't be able to drink many of these and stay focused on the goal at hand.

"So you made it in," I murmured. "Whose invitation did you steal?"

"I was about to ask you the same thing." Though his voice was light, his dark eyes danced with concern. "I guess I don't have to ask why you're here."

I waved the fan in front of my face, hiding my lips from any onlookers. "I'm here for the same reason you are."

"It's dangerous for you. More so than for me. But I'm sure I don't need to remind you of that."

"No," I snapped. "You don't."

"Anna, whatever you're intending, don't do it. There's already a plan in place and one that's most likely much better than yours."

Anger raged through me. His words felt like a challenge, as if I couldn't save my brother on my own. Granted, Branthe had a lot of rebels working for him as opposed to my one-man army.

Then I thought about how he dismissed me that night, how I knew he wanted to be together, but disregarded his own feelings. I looked at him then, studying those dark eyes. Part of me wanted to run away and not ask, but I couldn't help it.

"Has anything changed or do you still deny your feelings?"

His eyes widened, even behind the mask. I'd caught him off guard. Smug arrogance overtook me. At the same time, I noticed Colonel Mann all alone, his female cohort having disappeared. I looked around to see her on the arm of another man. Perfect. He wouldn't be seeing any more of her tonight.

"If you'll excuse me, I have work to do." Emboldened, I walked toward the colonel, not bothering to look back.

CHAPTER TWENTY

"If you haven't tried the rum punch, it's quite delicious," I said, lowering my voice in what I thought to be a seductive tone. Hopefully it seemed seductive enough that he didn't recognize it.

Shifty eyes scoured what he could see of my face and body. I made sure the bosom of the dress was cut low, not indecently so, but enough so to get a man's attention.

Focusing on my cleavage instead of my eyes, Mann replied, "I haven't had a nip, though if a woman as lovely as you is bringing it to me, I'll happily oblige." I handed him my glass and watched as he took a careful sip. Then another. Then he downed the whole thing. "Mmm. Yes, it's quite tasty." His seedy eyes rested back on my face. "Tell me, how is it a beautiful woman like yourself doesn't have a gentleman on her arm?"

Without cringing, I wrapped my hand around his bicep. "I do have one."

He giggled, sounding like a wheezing pig. "Oh well, then, my dear, let's get to know each other better."

"I couldn't agree more," I said. "But first, let's get more punch."

I spent the next two hours charming Colonel Mann like I'd charmed no other. It was working, too. His eyes soon became bleary, his focus erratic and a yawn came over him once or twice. After dowsing him with enough punch to put a horse down, I made my move.

Touching the brass buttons on his coat, I said, "It seems the party is dying down. I'll have to be leaving soon."

"Oh?" He swiped a finger over the top of my breasts. I wanted to vomit. "Don't do that. I have a room. You can stay and chat for a little while, can't you?"

"Of course." I smiled.

Teetering, he led me through the halls of the mansion. Acutely aware that anyone could see us together, especially Branthe, I constantly looked over my shoulder, expecting to be followed. But every time I looked, no one was there.

"Now which door is it?" he asked no one, pulling a key ring from his waistcoat. The ring! That had to be where he kept the key to Colvin's cage. But that couldn't be assumed. As much as the thought revolted me, he would have to be searched to make sure there were no other keys on him.

Finding it after what seemed an eternity, he put the key in the lock. I heard the ever-familiar click and he opened the door. Looking over my shoulder to make sure no one saw me, I followed him inside.

It was a basic room with a bed, desk and closet. The furnishings were covered with luxurious silks and velvets, but the colors were rather simple, tan and beige with ivory trimmings. Throwing his keys on the desk, he turned to me.

"Shall we keep the masks on or off?" he asked.

A cold shiver ran up my spine. "On." I tried to say it soothingly, as if I was genuinely attracted to him, but it came out stilted. Doing my best to cover up my disgust, I added, "Don't you think it's much more dangerous that way? Much more interesting?"

"Yes, I suppose it is." He giggled, sat on the bed and patted the place beside him. "Why don't you come over here?"

As soon as I sat down, he pawed at me. His thick lips nuzzled my neck, leaving a trail of saliva down my skin. My lips tightened. I could withstand this. For Colvin I could withstand almost anything. But when his hand shoved down my bodice, that was it. Reaching for one of the heavy candlesticks on the nightstand beside me, I bashed Mann over the head.

With all the drink he'd been given, I expected him to go down without much fight.

"What are you doing, you bitch?"

Wrong. He grabbed my hand and threw the candlestick on the floor. Forcing me down on the bed, he ripped the mask off my face. Mann laughed.

"Anna, I should've known you'd try something stupid. Thought you'd get a little revenge for what happened, did you?" Though his breath smelled like stale alcohol, he had his wits about him and I knew this time, he wouldn't let me get away.

CHAPTER TWENTY-ONE

I considered screaming, but knew it wouldn't help me. Anyone who came to my rescue would see a kitchen maid dressed up as a lady — a wanted kitchen maid at that. My fate would be even worse than simply being locked in the room with the colonel.

He ripped at my bodice. I fought him off, struggling to keep his fat, clumsy hands off me.

"Remember that inspection I didn't get to? Third time's the charm, eh? Well you're going to be inspected all over, girl, for what you've done. Every hole you've got is going to be prodded. Before I'm finished, you're going to wish you'd stayed far away from me."

I tried to push him off but he pulled back his arm and punched me in the belly. All wind left me. I gasped for air, trying to think through the shock of it. Unable to fight, Mann lifted up my skirts, thrusting his hand between my legs.

The shock of his touch brought me back and I kicked him in the gut. He staggered. At this point, two choices occurred to me — I could run or I could hit him again and hope that this time he was knocked out. Choice number two seemed logical.

I reached for the candlestick but he beat me to it and swung it at me. I managed to dodge the blow, but only by slipping off the bed and scrambling for the far wall.

"The next swing will hit you square across the face. You'll lose teeth. It might even break your jaw. Either way, you won't be going anywhere after that. So why don't you decide to play nice?"

"I'd rather die."

"You may have your wish." He swung the candlestick and at the same time I ducked, barreling into his middle. Mann lifted off his feet and fell on his back to the floor, me with him. I reached for his keys and felt hands around my neck.

I struggled to breath. Forgetting everything but the will to live, I tried to pry his hands from me. It was useless. His fingers gripped me like steel as panic set in. I couldn't breathe. I needed air. Lifting my hands to his neck, I tried to do the same to him but all ability to focus vanished. Thinking became impossible. It occurred to me that I'd die here, in the same room with a man I despised.

"I highly suggest you stop strangling my fiancé."

That voice. Branthe. He stood in the doorway. For some very odd reason, his request worked. Mann released me. I rolled off him, sputtering and heaving to catch air.

"She's not your fiancé. She's nothing more than a kitchen wench here to get her revenge on me," Mann spat.

"I assure you, she's my fiancé and whatever quarrel she has with you is deserved after what I've seen."

He just stood there. In the doorway. As if he owned the place. Branthe wasn't rattled, he wasn't worried, he simply *was*. In that moment, I realized I loved him. That I wished truly with my entire being that I was his fiancé because I wanted to spend every waking and sleeping moment with him, no matter what.

Mann's face paled. It was an odd reaction and I didn't understand until he spoke. "Andrews, you've got it all wrong."

Andrews, as in Lord Andrews? Surely not. Surely this whole time the man I'd been throwing myself at wasn't one of the great new government's loyal lords, given such titles because of their absolute fidelity to the Patriot Party.

"I don't have *anything* wrong and when the council discovers the man they've put in charge of rehabilitating morally corrupt criminals is himself nothing more than a rapist, they won't look too kindly on the rest of your career, of that you can be assured."

"But I—"

"There is one way to fix all this," Branthe continued, cool as ever, not reacting at all to Mann's bumbling attempt to save face. "Drop the charges against her. All charges. Every one. And no one will ever know what you've attempted here," he said as he gave Mann a hard stare, *"or in the past."*

Branthe meant what Mann would've done to me when I was a prisoner as well as what he'd already done to countless others. There was no telling what the man's sins were.

"Do we have a deal?"

Mann gave me a quick glance, one that said he was resigned to follow his fate. "We have a deal."

"Good. Luckily, my lawyer is attending the party. I'll have him draw up the papers right now. In the morning, you and your men will leave. I won't see your face again. Come, Anna."

He didn't have to tell me twice. I took his arm and left Colonel Mann behind me, never to be seen again. Though it was the happiest moment of my life, it was shadowed by the fact that I'd failed my brother, and now he would die.

CHAPTER TWENTY-TWO

Branthe led me to another room. His room, obviously, from the dark oak of the furniture and the sage green walls. He sat me down on the bed and crossed to a chair diagonal from me, sitting as well. He placed an ankle on his knee, his silk breeches looking soft enough to swim in under the candlelight.

"I asked you not to go along with your plan," he said, rubbing his tired face.

"And I never promised you I wouldn't."

He gave me a weary smile. "You could've gotten killed. Or worse."

It struck me what he'd done. That in one moment, this man had changed my life. "Thank you."

"For what?"

"For freeing me."

He looked down, smiling. "I don't know if I'd say that. I may have freed you from one thing, but I've bound you to another."

Bound me? Dear Lord, he meant the engagement. "But you only said that to save me from him."

He cocked an eyebrow. "Did I?"

"Didn't you?"

He drummed his fingers on the chair's armrest. "I'm not in the habit of saying things I don't mean."

So he meant it? It didn't seem real. My brain was clouded. I didn't come here to be distracted by this. There was Colvin to think about. "But my brother. He's still caged outside."

He shook his head. "Already taken care of. I told you we had a plan. When the colonel's men wake up, they'll find him mysteriously gone. Mann will have a hard enough time explaining that to his superiors. If he had that to deal with plus the scandal of what he was about to do to you, his career would be finished."

My mouth was dry. "So you saved Colvin?"

"My men did. Let me explain something to you, Anna. Now that you know who I am, I can finally tell you. Before, when you didn't know, I couldn't risk putting you or myself in any danger. You still haven't accepted my proposal, so I'm not sure if I should be telling you any of this."

"Branthe…" It was the first time I dared to say his name out loud. It scared me to do so, but it slipped from my tongue before I could stop it.

His sharp eyes darkened. "Branthe was my brother. He died several years ago. I was a loyal patriot before that happened. But when I discovered they'd burned and desecrated his body, I took his place as a rebel, using my patriotic stance as cover." He paused for a moment, looking away. "I'm Edward. I should've told you who I was but in some ways,

I wanted to keep the spirit of my brother alive, since he saved you so long ago. I'm sorry I couldn't reveal myself to you. Not before."

He looked crushed. I'd loved Branthe, a myth of a man, for most of my life. He was a man I didn't know, only one held close by my memories. This man, Edward, the one sitting before me, I knew. I'd spoken to him, laughed with him and was saved by him. He'd done more for me than his phantom brother ever had.

I loved him. I did.

"You couldn't ask for my hand before because I was wanted. As a patriot, you couldn't be tied to someone who was thought to be a rebel supporter."

He nodded. Before I even realized what he was doing, he crossed to me and took my hands in his. "You don't know how hard it was that night. I wanted you more than I've ever wanted anything my entire life. I would've asked you then, but I couldn't. I couldn't do anything until your name was cleared. Anna, I've never met anyone with more strength or defiance than you. I think I've loved you since the moment I first saw you in the forest and wanted to make you mine ever since then. Your name is now cleared. Will you marry me?"

There was only one answer. "Yes."

EPILOGUE

Three months later, I found myself standing on the balcony outside Edward's room. Looking out over Old Town, I knew my world wasn't perfect, but it was mine. There were many injustices, among them the virginity test for young women. It was something Edward promised to fight alongside me. Covertly, of course, but fight it nonetheless.

All these thoughts ran through my head as a hand squeezed my shoulder.

"Penny for the thoughts of my new bride."

I turned to see the smiling face of my husband. Still wearing his black waistcoat and breeches, I wrapped my arms around his middle. "I was thinking that even with how happy I am, I'm sorry Colvin couldn't be here."

He kissed my forehead. "He's safe. In fact," he said, leading me back to the bedroom, "he's working on our little project."

My eyebrows lifted. "He is? He's trying to stop the Rendering."

"He is, but you didn't hear that from me." He sighed. "Speaking of testing nether regions..." His eyes twinkled at me.

I eyed the bed and smiled. "Yes, I'm ready."

He pulled me to him. "Then let's begin married life," Edward murmured, kissing my neck.

"Yes, let's."

The End

Thank you for reading *An Unlikely Rebel*. If you enjoyed it, ***tell others*** about it or ***review*** it at Amazon or Goodreads. If you do write a review, please let me know at

amyboylesauthor@gmail.com

so I can personally thank you.

Amy Boyles

About the author:

Amy Boyles lives in North Alabama with her husband and has a passion for cooking ridiculously fattening food. She loves to be contacted by readers.

Connect with Me Online:
Website:
https://amyboylesauthor.wordpress.com
Twitter: http://twitter.com/amyboylesauthor
Facebook: http://facebook.com/amyboylesauthor

Don't miss the next chapters in The Dark Revolution – *Rendered* and *Baited*, now available. You can also get all three in a boxed set. Read on for an excerpt.

Rendered

The age of fifteen is usually one of discovery. So it was for Drian Becker. For at this age, she first witnessed the Rendering. It proved a sight she'd never forget.

"Adrian, I have something to show you," her father had said.

"What's that?" she asked, stepping carefully down the foyer stairs of their old colonial home, being sure not to get the fabric of the full length skirt under her slippered feet. Since the Patriot Party's mandate of full length skirts and corsets in the previous year, 2087, Drian had worn them everyday, though it still took practice not to step on the skirt's hem.

"Don't you look pretty," her father said, kissing her on the cheek.

"Thank you," she replied, trying not to sulk at her wardrobe. "You have something to show me."

He smiled, his bluebird eyes shining. "I do. I want you to see about that little idea you had."

She gulped. That little idea had been a joke, not meant to become institution-standard. Forcing a smile, she replied, "Yes, take me to see it." There was no other response. Anything else made her look like a traitor, and she wasn't a traitor.

With all the oil gone, making automobiles useless, the two piled into the black antique carriage her father acquired from a local museum. Matching chestnut mares and a driver wearing a black coat and breeches chauffeured them the half day's ride to Brenton.

Construction on the outer wall of the city looked to be full speed ahead. Made of a combination of wood and steel, patriots hammered and sawed the pieces into place. This small city in western Tennessee was to become the first fort in the new government. Most of the older forts being located so far from towns that they were useless. People needed protection - from rebels and themselves, as the new government said. Because of that, the standing army needed to remain close. So close it gave Drian the creeps.

The carriage whisked through the gates and down the asphalt streets. Potholes lined the way left and right, and once or twice the wheels struck one.

"Those were supposed to have been fixed," her father complained. "I'll make sure they are for the next time."

Drian said nothing, only watched the small city through the window of the carriage. After half an hour of starting and stopping at each and every intersection, they arrived at an old metal building. Rust lined the steel roof plates in streams, running down the top and onto the sides. The windows were coated in dirt so thick she couldn't see in but the door, oh that was something to see. Brand new with a fresh coat of stain, the oak door looked out of place among the ruins of the rest of the building.

"Come on, we're going inside."

She followed her father demurely, not sure if she really wanted to see what lay on the other side of that door. But what choice did she have? Saying no always meant the same thing - traitor.

He rapped the door a few times with his gold handled cane. A prop that was only for show, Drian noted, and made him appear much older than he was. But he liked it. He liked all of it - the clothes, the backwards way of living, the power it afforded him.

The door swung open. A young man, a captain from the looks of the ribbons on the breast of his redcoat, greeted him with a warm smile. "Commander, we've been expecting you."

"I hope you didn't start without me, Reynolds. I've brought someone special," he said, nodding toward Drian.

"Oh, the young man replied. "Is she to be rendered?"

Drian swallowed. Was she? Her father hadn't said as much. God, she hoped not.

"No," he snapped. "She's my guest. Now let us in."

The man named Reynolds stepped back as her father ushered himself inside. She gave a quick nod to the captain and squeaked in behind him.

The place was dark. Affixed to the wall hung candles and lanterns, yet the inside still possessed an eerie darkness that made Drian shiver. She wedged close to her father, practically clutching his coat as they walked through the warehouse.

"Stay close," he said. "You don't want to get separated in here."

She didn't have to be told twice. Drian glanced around as he led her through what must have been a hallway, but felt like tunnel. The myriad of lanterns and candles made the enclosure sweltering. Perspiration lined her forehead and trickled down her temples, though part of it might have simply been nerves.

Finally, the tunnel opened into what could only be described as an observation deck. The semi-circular room, lined with stacked seating, overlooked a wall of glass. A group of men stood at the glass, all in uniform, and all looking down at something. Timidity getting the better of her, Drian shuffled her feet, hoping to take one of the seats in the back.

"Come. This is what we're here for," her father demanded.

But something told her not to go. Something told her to stay far, far away from that glass. She tried, her feet moving without command in the opposite direction. But her father grabbed her hand and growled in her ear.

"You will not make me look a fool."

He led her front and center, creating a hole in the observers already stationed there.

"Commander," most of them murmured.

"Gentlemen," my father replied. "I've brought a special treat for you today - my daughter. The creator of the Rendering. If it wasn't for her brilliance, we wouldn't be here and the Patriot Party wouldn't have the same hold as it does."

The men, most of them around her father's age, glanced at her with what could only have been described as reverence. Drian gulped. She felt like a china doll on display, scrutinized under the bushy eyebrows of these men.

Her father placed a hand on each shoulder. She thought (it was rather a ridiculous) that his intention was to hold her there so that she couldn't run. Just because she felt claustrophobic and slightly overwhelmed didn't mean she wanted to run. Neither did the line of sweat running down her back make her want to run. But what did make her want to run were the looks on the men's faces.

They looked like dogs with bones just out of reach. Their eyes glistened, their lips smacked. Need and want washed over their faces like a grotesque mask at a horrible masquerade party. It wasn't until Drian finally looked down below, observing what she was there to observe, that she understood.

At least three dozen lanterns flourished around the room, washing the place with a golden glow. Lying on a steel table, in the center of this makeshift arena, was a woman. Not any woman - a young one, perhaps fifteen or so - the same age as Drian. Four men, much older, stood in front of her.

Her feet were pushed squarely into two stirrups at the end of the bed, while her head rested on a cushion. The first man, wearing rubber gloves, said something to her and she shimmied down the table, closer to him. When he seemed satisfied with her position, he lifted her skirts, handing them to her.

The girl lay naked below the waist before these four men. The first man, using some sort of small steel instrument that was shaped sort of like a pencil but with a small disk on one end, slowly inserted it into her. The girl tensed for a moment while the thing was inside her but then relaxed when he pulled it out.

He said something to the man beside him and stepped out of the way. This second man, Drian recognized. Judge Walter Thomas, known for steep punishments on minor (or what used to be minor) offenses. Take a man's daily ration of food and you'd get the tip of your pinky sliced off. *Sell* a man your daily ration of food and you'd lose the whole finger. And that was even if you gave up the food. It was your ration - you needed to eat it - not wait in line for it and then sell it to someone else.

Judge Thomas was old, around fifty or so with sagging jowls and a belly so big she knew he hadn't seen his feet in years. Nevertheless, the extra weight didn't stop him now. Without hesitation, he inserted a finger inside the girl, as if corroborating what the first man (a doctor, most like) had diagnosed.

But the judge didn't just insert his finger and remove it, like his predecessor had done with the instrument. No, he moved it in and out a few times as if he enjoyed it. He did that for maybe half a minute while the girl lay there, unmoving. Finally, he pulled his finger out and with the same hand, reached up and squeezed her breast.

Inside the room, a man snickered. Drian didn't see who.

The judge stepped back and the third man took his place between the girl's legs. He did the same thing as the judge, but only for a brief second. He then nodded to the doctor.

The last man, holding a clipboard and writing stylus, scribbled down a few things and then said something to the men. The doctor lowered the girl's skirts and helped her off the table. The scribe then escorted her from the room, leaving the three men alone. A few seconds later, he returned with a new girl.

Drian saw enough. She turned away. "Thank you for bringing me," she said to her father. "I understand the work you're doing. I see it's very important." Her voice wasn't convincing, she knew that, but it was the best she could muster.

"Do you?" he asked, arching an eyebrow. "That first girl will be matched well. She is intact and remained docile through the examination. The party will ensure she finds a good husband."

"Glad to hear it," she replied, a knot twisting inside her stomach. "I've seen enough."

"But this is your work. Your idea. Don't you want to see more."

She shook her head.

"Very well," he said, stamping the cane to the ground. "We'll leave."

Drian followed him back out of the room and through the dark maze. The hallway felt smaller, as if it was closing in on her. Her head felt light. She tried to breathe deeply but the damn corset around her waist forbade it.

Finally, they reached the outside. Drian tumbled from the building, her father barely catching her before she hit the ground.

"It's not my work," she mumbled. "I didn't do that."

He held her, stroking a bit of hair from her face. "But it is your work and it's good work. It's what the country needs."

He helped her into the carriage. She sat at the window, numbly watching the scenery pass by as they entered the streets. *It's good work*, he'd said.

No. She thought. This isn't my work and I'll do everything I can to stop it. No matter what.

UNLIKELY REBEL

Amy Boyles